WILLIAM SHAKESPEARE was born in Stratford-upon-Avon in April, 1564, and his birth is traditionally celebrated on April 23. The facts of his life, known from surviving documents, are sparse. He was one of eight children born to John Shakespeare, a merchant of some standing in his community. William probably went to the King's New School in Stratford, but he had no university education. In November 1582, at the age of eighteen, he married Anne Hathaway, eight years his senior, who was pregnant with their first child, Susanna. She was born on May 26, 1583. Twins, a boy, Hamnet (who would die at age eleven), and a girl, Judith, were born in 1585. By 1592 Shakespeare had gone to London, working as an actor and already known as a playwright. A rival dramatist, Robert Greene, referred to him as "an upstart crow, beautified with our feathers." Shakespeare became a principal shareholder and playwright of the successful acting troupe the Lord Chamberlain's men (later, under James I, called the King's men). In 1599 the Lord Chamberlain's men built and occupied the Globe Theatre in Southwark near the Thames River. Here many of Shakespeare's plays were performed by the most famous actors of his time, including Richard Burbage, Will Kempe, and Robert Armin. In addition to his 37 plays, Shakespeare had a hand in others, including *Sir Thomas More* and *The Two Noble Kinsmen*, and he wrote poems, including *Venus and Adonis* and *The Rape of Lucrece*. His 154 sonnets were published, probably without his authorization, in 1609. In 1611 or 1612 he gave up his lodgings in London and devoted more and more of his time to retirement in Stratford, though he continued writing such plays as *The Tempest* and *Henry VIII* until about 1613. He died on April 23, 1616, and was buried in Holy Trinity Church, Stratford. No collected edition of his plays was published during his lifetime, but in 1623 two members of his acting company, John Heminges and Henry Condell, published the great collection now called the First Folio.

Bantam Shakespeare
The Complete Works—29 Volumes
Edited by David Bevington
With forewords by Joseph Papp on the plays

The Poems: Venus and Adonis, The Rape of Lucrece, The
Phoenix and Turtle, A Lover's Complaint,
the Sonnets

Antony and Cleopatra	*The Merchant of Venice*
As You Like It	*A Midsummer Night's Dream*
The Comedy of Errors	*Much Ado about Nothing*
Hamlet	*Othello*
Henry IV, Part One	*Richard II*
Henry IV, Part Two	*Richard III*
Henry V	*Romeo and Juliet*
Julius Caesar	*The Taming of the Shrew*
King Lear	*The Tempest*
Macbeth	*Twelfth Night*

Together in one volume:

Henry VI, Parts One, Two, and Three
King John and Henry VIII
Measure for Measure, All's Well that Ends Well, and
Troilus and Cressida
Three Early Comedies: Love's Labor's Lost, The Two
Gentlemen of Verona, The Merry
Wives of Windsor
Three Classical Tragedies: Titus Andronicus, Timon
of Athens, Coriolanus
The Late Romances: Pericles, Cymbeline, The Winter's
Tale, The Tempest

Two collections:

Four Comedies: The Taming of the Shrew, A Midsummer
Night's Dream, The Merchant of Venice,
Twelfth Night
Four Tragedies: Hamlet, Othello, King Lear, Macbeth

William Shakespeare

JULIUS CAESAR

Edited by
David Bevington

David Scott Kastan,
James Hammersmith,
and Robert Kean Turner,
Associate Editors

With a Foreword by
Joseph Papp

BANTAM BOOKS
NEW YORK · TORONTO · LONDON · SYDNEY · AUCKLAND

JULIUS CAESAR
A Bantam Book / published by arrangement with Scott, Foresman and Company

PUBLISHING HISTORY

Scott, Foresman edition published / January 1980
Bantam edition, with newly edited text and substantially revised, edited, and amplified notes,
introductions, and other materials, published / February 1988
Valuable advice on staging matters has been provided by Richard Hosley.
Collations checked by Eric Rasmussen.
Additional editorial assistance by Claire McEachern.

ISBN 0-553-21296-6

Published simultaneously in the United States and Canada

Bantam Books are published by Bantam Books, a division of Bantam Doubleday Dell Publishing Group,
Inc. Its trademark, consisting of the words "Bantam Books" and the portrayal of a rooster, is Registered
in U.S. Patent and Trademark Office and in other countries. Marca Registrada. Bantam Books, 1540
Broadway, New York, New York 10036.

PRINTED IN THE UNITED STATES OF ···

OPM   20 19 18 17

Contents

Foreword   vii

Introduction   xvii

Julius Caesar
  in Performance   xxv

The Playhouse   xxxi

JULIUS CAESAR   1

Date and Text   103

Textual Notes   104

Shakespeare's Sources   105

Further Reading   131

Memorable Lines   135

Foreword

It's hard to imagine, but Shakespeare wrote all of his plays with a quill pen, a goose feather whose hard end had to be sharpened frequently. How many times did he scrape the dull end to a point with his knife, dip it into the inkwell, and bring up, dripping wet, those wonderful words and ideas that are known all over the world?

In the age of word processors, typewriters, and ballpoint pens, we have almost forgotten the meaning of the word "blot." Yet when I went to school, in the 1930s, my classmates and I knew all too well what an inkblot from the metal-tipped pens we used would do to a nice clean page of a test paper, and we groaned whenever a splotch fell across the sheet. Most of us finished the school day with ink-stained fingers; those who were less careful also went home with ink-stained shirts, which were almost impossible to get clean.

When I think about how long it took me to write the simplest composition with a metal-tipped pen and ink, I can only marvel at how many plays Shakespeare scratched out with his goose-feather quill pen, year after year. Imagine him walking down one of the narrow cobblestoned streets of London, or perhaps drinking a pint of beer in his local alehouse. Suddenly his mind catches fire with an idea, or a sentence, or a previously elusive phrase. He is burning with impatience to write it down—but because he doesn't have a ballpoint pen or even a pencil in his pocket, he has to keep the idea in his head until he can get to his quill and parchment.

He rushes back to his lodgings on Silver Street, ignoring the vendors hawking brooms, the coaches clattering by, the piteous wails of beggars and prisoners. Bounding up the stairs, he snatches his quill and starts to write furiously, not even bothering to light a candle against the dusk. "To be, or not to be," he scrawls, "that is the—." But the quill point has gone dull, the letters have fattened out illegibly, and in the middle of writing one of the most famous passages in the history of dramatic literature, Shakespeare has to stop to sharpen his pen.

Taking a deep breath, he lights a candle now that it's dark, sits down, and begins again. By the time the candle has burned out and the noisy apprentices of his French Huguenot landlord have quieted down, Shakespeare has finished Act 3 of *Hamlet* with scarcely a blot.

Early the next morning, he hurries through the fog of a London summer morning to the rooms of his colleague Richard Burbage, the actor for whom the role of Hamlet is being written. He finds Burbage asleep and snoring loudly, sprawled across his straw mattress. Not only had the actor performed in *Henry V* the previous afternoon, but he had then gone out carousing all night with some friends who had come to the performance.

Shakespeare shakes his friend awake, until, bleary-eyed, Burbage sits up in his bed. "Dammit, Will," he grumbles, "can't you let an honest man sleep?" But the playwright, his eyes shining and the words tumbling out of his mouth, says, "Shut up and listen—tell me what you think of *this*!"

He begins to read to the still half-asleep Burbage, pacing around the room as he speaks. ". . . Whether 'tis nobler in the mind to suffer the slings and arrows of outrageous fortune—"

Burbage interrupts, suddenly wide awake, "That's excellent, very good, 'the slings and arrows of outrageous fortune,' yes, I think it will work quite well. . . ." He takes the parchment from Shakespeare and murmurs the lines to himself, slowly at first but with growing excitement.

The sun is just coming up, and the words of one of Shakespeare's most famous soliloquies are being uttered for the first time by the first actor ever to bring Hamlet to life. It must have been an exhilarating moment.

Shakespeare wrote most of his plays to be performed live by the actor Richard Burbage and the rest of the Lord Chamberlain's men (later the King's men). Today, however, our first encounter with the plays is usually in the form of the printed word. And there is no question that reading Shakespeare for the first time isn't easy. His plays aren't comic books or magazines or the dime-store detective novels I read when I was young. A lot of his sentences are complex. Many of his words are no longer used in our everyday speech. His profound thoughts are often condensed into poetry, which is not as straightforward as prose.

Yet when you hear the words spoken aloud, a lot of the language may strike you as unexpectedly modern. For Shakespeare's plays, like any dramatic work, weren't really meant to be read; they were meant to be spoken, seen, and performed. It's amazing how lines that are so troublesome in print can flow so naturally and easily when spoken.

I think it was precisely this music that first fascinated me. When I was growing up, Shakespeare was a stranger to me. I had no particular interest in him, for I was from a different cultural tradition. It never occurred to me that his plays might be more than just something to "get through" in school, like science or math or the physical education requirement we had to fulfill. My passions then were movies, radio, and vaudeville—certainly not Elizabethan drama.

I was, however, fascinated by words and language. Because I grew up in a home where Yiddish was spoken, and English was only a second language, I was acutely sensitive to the musical sounds of different languages and had an ear for lilt and cadence and rhythm in the spoken word. And so I loved reciting poems and speeches even as a very young child. In first grade I learned lots of short nature verses— "Who has seen the wind?," one of them began. My first foray into drama was playing the role of Scrooge in Charles Dickens's *A Christmas Carol* when I was eight years old. I liked summoning all the scorn and coldness I possessed and putting them into the words, "Bah, humbug!"

From there I moved on to longer and more famous poems and other works by writers of the 1930s. Then, in junior high school, I made my first acquaintance with Shakespeare through his play *Julius Caesar*. Our teacher, Miss McKay, assigned the class a passage to memorize from the opening scene of the play, the one that begins "Wherefore rejoice? What conquest brings he home?" The passage seemed so wonderfully theatrical and alive to me, and the experience of memorizing and reciting it was so much fun, that I went on to memorize another speech from the play on my own.

I chose Mark Antony's address to the crowd in Act 3,

scene 2, which struck me then as incredibly high drama. Even today, when I speak the words, I feel the same thrill I did that first time. There is the strong and athletic Antony descending from the raised pulpit where he has been speaking, right into the midst of a crowded Roman square. Holding the torn and bloody cloak of the murdered Julius Caesar in his hand, he begins to speak to the people of Rome:

> If you have tears, prepare to shed them now.
> You all do know this mantle. I remember
> The first time ever Caesar put it on;
> 'Twas on a summer's evening in his tent,
> That day he overcame the Nervii.
> Look, in this place ran Cassius' dagger through.
> See what a rent the envious Casca made.
> Through this the well-belovèd Brutus stabbed,
> And as he plucked his cursèd steel away,
> Mark how the blood of Caesar followed it,
> As rushing out of doors to be resolved
> If Brutus so unkindly knocked or no;
> For Brutus, as you know, was Caesar's angel.
> Judge, O you gods, how dearly Caesar loved him!
> This was the most unkindest cut of all . . .

I'm not sure now that I even knew Shakespeare had written a lot of other plays, or that he was considered "timeless," "universal," or "classic"—but I knew a good speech when I heard one, and I found the splendid rhythms of Antony's rhetoric as exciting as anything I'd ever come across.

Fifty years later, I still feel that way. Hearing good actors speak Shakespeare gracefully and naturally is a wonderful experience, unlike any other I know. There's a satisfying fullness to the spoken word that the printed page just can't convey. This is why seeing the plays of Shakespeare performed live in a theater is the best way to appreciate them. If you can't do that, listening to sound recordings or watching film versions of the plays is the next best thing.

But if you do start with the printed word, use the play as a script. Be an actor yourself and say the lines out loud. Don't worry too much at first about words you don't immediately understand. Look them up in the footnotes or a dictionary, but don't spend too much time on this. It is more profitable (and fun) to get the sense of a passage and sing it out. Speak naturally, almost as if you were talking to a friend, but be sure to enunciate the words properly. You'll be surprised at how much you understand simply by speaking the speech "trippingly on the tongue," as Hamlet advises the Players.

You might start, as I once did, with a speech from *Julius Caesar*, in which the tribune (city official) Marullus scolds the commoners for transferring their loyalties so quickly from the defeated and murdered general Pompey to the newly victorious Julius Caesar:

> Wherefore rejoice? What conquest brings he home?
> What tributaries follow him to Rome
> To grace in captive bonds his chariot wheels?
> You blocks, you stones, you worse than senseless
> things!
> O you hard hearts, you cruel men of Rome,
> Knew you not Pompey? Many a time and oft
> Have you climbed up to walls and battlements,
> To towers and windows, yea, to chimney tops,
> Your infants in your arms, and there have sat
> The livelong day, with patient expectation,
> To see great Pompey pass the streets of Rome.

With the exception of one or two words like "wherefore" (which means "why," not "where"), "tributaries" (which means "captives"), and "patient expectation" (which means patient waiting), the meaning and emotions of this speech can be easily understood.

From here you can go on to dialogues or other more challenging scenes. Although you may stumble over unaccustomed phrases or unfamiliar words at first, and even fall flat when you're crossing some particularly rocky passages, pick yourself up and stay with it. Remember that it takes time to feel at home with anything new. Soon you'll come to recognize Shakespeare's unique sense of humor and way of saying things as easily as you recognize a friend's laughter.

And then it will just be a matter of choosing which one of Shakespeare's plays you want to tackle next. As a true fan of his, you'll find that you're constantly learning from his plays. It's a journey of discovery that you can continue for the rest of your life. For no matter how many times you read or see a particular play, there will always be something new there that you won't have noticed before.

Why do so many thousands of people get hooked on Shakespeare and develop a habit that lasts a lifetime? What can he really say to us today, in a world filled with inventions and problems he never could have imagined? And how do you get past his special language and difficult sentence structure to understand him?

The best way to answer these questions is to go see a live production. You might not know much about Shakespeare, or much about the theater, but when you watch actors performing one of his plays on the stage, it will soon become clear to you why people get so excited about a playwright who lived hundreds of years ago.

For the story—what's happening in the play—is the most accessible part of Shakespeare. In *A Midsummer Night's Dream*, for example, you can immediately understand the situation: a girl is chasing a guy who's chasing a girl who's chasing another guy. No wonder *A Midsummer Night's Dream* is one of the most popular of Shakespeare's plays: it's about one of the world's most popular pastimes—falling in love.

But the course of true love never did run smooth, as the young suitor Lysander says. Often in Shakespeare's comedies the girl whom the guy loves doesn't love him back, or she loves him but he loves someone else. In *The Two Gentlemen of Verona*, Julia loves Proteus, Proteus loves Sylvia, and Sylvia loves Valentine, who is Proteus's best friend. In the end, of course, true love prevails, but not without lots of complications along the way.

For in all of his plays—comedies, histories, and tragedies—Shakespeare is showing you human nature. His characters act and react in the most extraordinary ways—and sometimes in the most incomprehensible ways. People are always trying to find motivations for what a character does. They ask, "Why does Iago want to destroy Othello?"

The answer, to me, is very simple—because that's the way Iago is. That's just his nature. Shakespeare doesn't explain his characters; he sets them in motion—and away they go. He doesn't worry about whether they're likable or not. He's interested in interesting people, and his most fascinating characters are those who are unpredictable. If you lean back in your chair early on in one of his plays, thinking you've figured out what Iago or Shylock (in *The Merchant of Venice*) is up to, don't be too sure—because that great judge of human nature, Shakespeare, will surprise you every time.

He is just as wily in the way he structures a play. In *Macbeth*, a comic scene is suddenly introduced just after the bloodiest and most treacherous slaughter imaginable, of a guest and king by his host and subject, when in comes a drunk porter who has to go to the bathroom. Shakespeare is tickling your emotions by bringing a stand-up comic on-stage right on the heels of a savage murder.

It has taken me thirty years to understand even some of these things, and so I'm not suggesting that Shakespeare is immediately understandable. I've gotten to know him not through theory but through practice, the practice of the *living* Shakespeare—the playwright of the theater.

Of course the plays are a great achievement of dramatic literature, and they should be studied and analyzed in schools and universities. But you must always remember, when reading all the words *about* the playwright and his plays, that *Shakespeare's* words came first and that in the end there is nothing greater than a single actor on the stage speaking the lines of Shakespeare.

Everything important that I know about Shakespeare comes from the practical business of producing and directing his plays in the theater. The task of classifying, criticizing, and editing Shakespeare's printed works I happily leave to others. For me, his plays really do live on the stage, not on the page. That is what he wrote them for and that is how they are best appreciated.

Although Shakespeare lived and wrote hundreds of years ago, his name rolls off my tongue as if he were my brother. As a producer and director, I feel that there is a professional relationship between us that spans the centuries. As a human being, I feel that Shakespeare has enriched my understanding of life immeasurably. I hope you'll let him do the same for you.

❖

Julius Caesar holds a special place in my heart as my first encounter with Shakespeare. I fell in love with the oratory, especially, as I've said before, the great speeches of Antony. "Friends, Romans, countrymen, lend me your ears," is probably the single most famous line in Shakespeare, with the possible exception of "O Romeo, Romeo, wherefore art thou Romeo?" There are many eloquent speeches throughout the play, especially the marvelous rhetoric of Mark Antony over the dead body of Caesar.

My favorite scene is the quarrel between Brutus and Cassius in Act 4, scene 3. Here the emotional nuances—guilt, accusation, defensiveness, anger, hurt—are so skillfully wrought that you can almost touch them. One of the finer moments in this great scene occurs after bitter words have passed between these comrades-in-arms, at the point where Brutus says, "Portia is dead." Cassius, who has been carrying on like a petulant child, painfully recognizes that Brutus had been bearing in his bosom the news of his own wife's death throughout the entire contretemps, and Cassius is filled with deep shame—"How scaped I killing when I crossed you so? / O insupportable and touching loss!"

I like Mark Antony for his passion and his loyalty to Caesar. Cassius I find interesting, but very childish. His petty competition with Caesar, and his hateful determination to bring Caesar down to his own level, makes his role less than honorable.

Frankly, I've never liked Brutus, because his ideals lack an emotional base and therefore become subject to rationalizations that justify the murder of Caesar. Even his remarks to his co-conspirators before they butcher Julius Caesar, though high sounding, lack compassion for the man who had befriended him: "Let's carve him as a dish fit for the gods, / Not hew him as a carcass fit for hounds." But no amount of intellectualization can obscure the fact that Brutus, as Antony tells the crowd, inflicted "the most unkindest cut of all."

JOSEPH PAPP

JOSEPH PAPP GRATEFULLY ACKNOWLEDGES THE HELP OF ELIZABETH KIRKLAND IN PREPARING THIS FOREWORD.

JULIUS
CAESAR

Introduction

Julius Caesar stands midway in Shakespeare's dramatic career, at a critical juncture. In some ways it is an epilogue to his English history plays of the 1590s; in other ways it introduces the period of the great tragedies. The play was evidently first performed at the new Globe Theater in the fall of 1599, shortly after *Henry V* (the last of Shakespeare's history plays about medieval England) and around the time of *As You Like It* (one of the last of Shakespeare's happy romantic comedies). It shortly preceded *Hamlet*. It is placed among the tragedies in the Folio of 1623, where it was first published, and is entitled *The Tragedy of Julius Caesar*, but in the table of contents it is listed as *The Life and Death of Julius Caesar* as though it were a history.

Julius Caesar shares with Shakespeare's history plays an absorption in the problems of civil war and popular unrest. Rome, like England, suffers an internal division that is reflected in the perturbed state of the heavens themselves. The commoners, or plebeians, are easily swayed by demagogues. Opportunists prosper in this atmosphere of crisis, although fittingly even they are sometimes undone by their own scheming. Politics seems to require a morality quite apart from that of personal life, posing a tragic dilemma for Brutus as it did for Richard II or Henry VI. The blending of history and tragedy in *Julius Caesar*, then, is not unlike that found in several English history plays. Rome was a natural subject to which Shakespeare might turn in his continuing depiction of human political behavior. Roman culture had recently been elevated to new importance by the classical orientation of the Renaissance. As a model of political organization it loomed larger in Elizabethan consciousness than it does in ours because so few other models were available, and because Greek culture was less accessible in language and tradition. According to a widely accepted mythology, Elizabethans considered themselves descended from the Romans through another Brutus, the great grandson of Aeneas.

Yet the differences between Roman and English history are as important as the similarities. Rome's choice during

her civil wars lay between a senatorial republican form
of government and a strong single ruler. Although the mon-
archical English might be inclined to be suspicious of republicanism, they had no experience to compare with it—
certainly not their various peasants' revolts such as Jack
Cade's rebellion (in *2 Henry VI*). On the other hand, Roman one-man rule as it flourished under Octavius Caesar
lacked the English sanctions of divine right and monarchi-
cal primogeniture. Rome was, after all, a pagan culture, and
Shakespeare carefully preserves this non-Christian frame
of reference. The gods are frequently invoked and appear to
respond with prophetic dreams and auguries, but their ultimate intentions are baffling. Humans strive blindly; the will of
the gods is inscrutable. The outcome of *Julius Caesar* is far
different from the restoration of providentially ordained order at the end of *Richard III*. Calm is restored and political
authority reestablished, but we are by no means sure that a
divine morality has been served. Roman history for Shakespeare is history divested of its divine imperatives and lo-
cated in a distant political setting, making dispassionate
appraisal less difficult. In Plutarch's *Lives of the Noble Grecians and Romans* as translated by Sir Thomas North,
Shakespeare discovered a rich opportunity for pursuing the
ironies of political life to which he had been increasingly
attracted in the English histories. In fact he was drawn
throughout his career to Plutarch: to the portrait of Portia
in "The Life of Marcus Brutus" not only for Portia in *Julius
Caesar* but for Lucrece in *The Rape of Lucrece*, Kate in
1 Henry IV, and Portia in *The Merchant of Venice;* to "The
Life of Theseus" for the Duke of *A Midsummer Night's
Dream;* and to various Lives for *Julius Caesar, Coriolanus,
Antony and Cleopatra,* and *Timon of Athens.* Freed from the
orthodoxies of the Elizabethan world view, Shakespeare
turned in the Roman or classical plays toward irony or out-
right satire (as in *Troilus and Cressida*) and toward the per-
sonal tragedy of political dilemma (as in *Coriolanus* and
Julius Caesar). These are to be the dominant motifs of the
Roman or classical plays, as distinguished from both the
English histories and the great tragedies of evil, in which
politics plays a lesser part (*Hamlet, Othello, King Lear,
Macbeth*).

Julius Caesar is an ambivalent study of civil conflict. As in *Richard II,* the play is structured around two protagonists rather than one. Caesar and Brutus, men of extraordinary abilities and debilitating weaknesses, are more like each other than either would care to admit. This antithetical balance reflects a dual tradition: the medieval view of Dante and Geoffrey Chaucer condemning Brutus and Cassius as conspirators, and the Renaissance view of Sir Philip Sidney and Ben Jonson condemning Caesar as a tyrant.

Caesar is a study in paradox. He is unquestionably a great general, astute in politics, decisive in his judgments, and sharp in his evaluation of men—as, for example, in his distrust of Cassius with his "lean and hungry look" (1.2.194). Yet this mightiest of men, who in Cassius' phrase bestrides the narrow world "Like a Colossus" (l. 136), is also deaf in one ear, prone to fevers and epilepsy, unable to compete with Cassius by swimming the Tiber fully armed, and afflicted with a sterile marriage. Physical limitations of this sort are common enough, but in Caesar they are constantly juxtaposed with his aspirations to be above mortal weakness. He dies boasting that he is like the "northern star," constant, unique, "Unshaked of motion" (3.1.61–71). He professes to fear nothing and yet is notoriously superstitious. He calmly reflects that "death, a necessary end, / Will come when it will come," and then arrogantly boasts in the next moment that "Danger knows full well / That Caesar is more dangerous than he" (2.2.36–45). As his wife puts it, Caesar's "wisdom is consumed in confidence" (l. 49). He willfully betrays his own best instincts and ignores plain warnings through self-deception. He stops a procession to hear a soothsayer and then dismisses the man as "a dreamer" (1.2.24). He commissions his augurers to determine whether he should stay at home on the ides of March and then persuades himself that acting on their advice would be a sign of weakness. Most fatally, he thinks himself above flattery and so is especially vulnerable to it. So wise and powerful a man as this cannot stop the process of his own fate, because his fate and character are interwoven: he is the victim of his own hubris. His insatiable desire for the crown overbalances his judgment; no warnings of the gods can save him. Even his virtues conspire against him, for he

regards himself as one who puts public interest ahead of
personal affairs and brushes aside the letter of Artemidorus that would have told him of the conspiracy.

Brutus, for all his opposition to Caesar, is also a paradoxi-
cal figure. His strengths are quite unlike those of Caesar,
but his weaknesses are surprisingly similar. Brutus is a noble Roman from an ancient family whose glory it has been
to defend the personal liberties of Rome, the republican tradition. Brutus' virtues are personal virtues. He enjoys an
admirable rapport with his courageous and intelligent wife
and is genuinely kind to his servants. In friendship he is
trustworthy. He deplores oaths in the conspiracy because
his word is his bond. He finds Caesar's ambition for power
distasteful and vulgar; his opposition to Caesar is both idealistic and patrician. Brutus' hubris is a pride of family,
and on this score he is vulnerable to flattery. As Cassius re-
minds him, alluding to Brutus' ancestor Lucius Junius Brutus, who founded the Roman Republic in 509 B.C.: "There
was a Brutus once that would have brooked / Th' eternal
devil to keep his state in Rome / As easily as a king"
(1.2.159–161). Should not Marcus Brutus be the savior of his
country from a return to tyranny? Is not he a more fit leader
for Rome than Caesar? " 'Brutus' and 'Caesar.' What should
be in that 'Caesar'? / Why should that name be sounded more
than yours?" (ll. 142–143). Cassius' strategy is to present to
Brutus numerous testimonials "all tending to the great opinion / That Rome holds of his name" (ll. 318–319). Cassius
plays the role of tempter here, but the notion he suggests is
not new to Brutus.

Cassius works on Brutus' pride much as, in a parallel and
adjoining scene, Decius works on Caesar's ambition (2.1 and
2.2). In these two scenes, the protagonists enter alone during
the troubled night, call for a servant, receive the conspirators, and dispute the wise caution of their wives. Both men
are predisposed to the temptations that are placed before
them. Brutus has often thought of himself as the indispens-
able man for the preservation of Rome's liberties. Despite his
good breeding and coolly rational manner, he is as dominating
a personality as Caesar, as hard to move once his mind is made
up. Indeed, the conspiracy founders on Brutus' repeated insistence on having his way. He allows no oaths among the conspirators and will not kill Antony along with Caesar. He

permits Antony to speak after him in Caesar's funeral. He vetoes Cicero as a fellow conspirator. In each instance the other conspirators are unanimously opposed to Brutus' choice but yield to him. Brutus cuts off Cassius' objections before hearing them fully, being accustomed to having his way without dispute. His motives are in part noble and idealistic: Brutus wishes to have the conspirators behave generously and openly, as heroes rather than as henchmen. Yet there is something loftily patrician in his desire to have the fruits of conspiracy without any of the dirty work. His willingness to have Antony speak after him betrays a vain confidence in his own oratory and an unjustified faith in the plebeian mob. Moreover, when Brutus overrides Cassius once more in the decision to fight at Philippi and is proved wrong by the event, no idealistic motive can excuse Brutus' insistence on being obeyed; Cassius is the more experienced soldier. Still, Brutus' fatal limitations as leader of a coup d'état are inseparable from his virtues as a private man. The truth is that such a noble man is, by his very nature, unsuited for the stern exigencies of assassination and civil war. Brutus is strong-minded about his ideals, but he cannot be ruthless. The means and the end of revolution drift further and further apart. He cannot supply his troops at Philippi because he will not forage among the peasants of the countryside and will not countenance among his allies the routine corruptions of an army in time of war—though at the same time that he upbraids Cassius for not sending him gold, he does not stop to ask where the gold would come from. Even suicide is distasteful for Brutus, obliging him to embarrass his friends by asking their help. Brutus is too high-minded and genteel a man for the troubled times in which he lives.

The times indeed seem to demand ruthless action of the sort Antony and Octavius are all too ready to provide. The greatest irony of Brutus' fall is that the coup he undertakes for Roman liberty yields only further diminutions of that liberty. The plebeians are not ready for the commonwealth Brutus envisages. From the first they are portrayed as amiable but "saucy" (even in the opinion of their tribunes, Flavius and Marullus). They adulate Caesar at the expense of their previous idol, Pompey. When Brutus successfully appeals for a moment to their changeable loyalties, they cry "Let him be Caesar," and "Caesar's better parts / Shall be crowned in

Brutus" (3.2.51–52). If Brutus were not swayed by this hero worship, he would have good cause to be disillusioned. To his credit he is not the demagogue the plebeians take him for and so cannot continue to bend them to his will. Cassius, too, for all his villainlike role as tempter to Brutus, his envious motive, and his Epicurean skepticism, reveals a finer nature as the play progresses. Inspired perhaps by Brutus' philosophic idealism, Cassius turns philosopher also and accepts defeat in a noble but ineffectual cause. Yet even his death is futile; Cassius is misinformed about the fate of his friend Titinius and so stabs himself just when the battle is going well for the conspirators.

The ultimate victors are Antony and Octavius. Antony, whatever finer nature he may possess, becomes under the stress of circumstance a cunning bargainer with the conspirators and a masterful rhetorician who characterizes himself to the plebeians as a "plain blunt man" (3.2.219). In sardonic soliloquy at the end of his funeral oration he observes, "Now let it work. Mischief, thou art afoot. / Take thou what course thou wilt" (ll. 261–262). He is, to be sure, stirred by loyalty to Caesar's memory, but to the end of avenging Caesar's death he is prepared to unleash violence at whatever risk to the state. He regards Lepidus contemptuously as a mere creature under his command. Antony is older than Octavius and teaches the younger man about political realities, but an Elizabethan audience would probably savor the irony that Octavius will subsequently beat Antony at his own game. At Philippi, Octavius' refusal to accept Antony's directions in the battle (5.1.16–20) gives us a glimpse of the peremptory manner for which he is to become famous, like his predecessor. Antony and Octavius together are in any case a fearsome pair, matter-of-factly noting down the names of those who must die, including their own kinsmen. They cut off the bequests left to the populace in Caesar's will (4.1), by which Antony had won the hearts of the plebeians. Many innocent persons are sacrificed in the new reign of terror, including Cicero and the poet unluckily named Cinna. In such deaths, art and civilization yield to expediency. Rationality gives way to frenzied rhetoric and to a struggle for power in which Rome's republican tradition is buried forever. Such is the achievement of Brutus' noble revolution.

Appropriately for such a depiction of ambivalent political

strife, *Julius Caesar* is written chiefly in the oratorical mode. It resembles its near contemporary, *Henry V,* in devoting so much attention to speeches of public persuasion. The famous orations following Caesar's assassination, one by Brutus in the so-called Laconic style (that is, concise and sententious) and one by Antony in the Asiatic style (that is, more florid, anecdotal, and literary), are only the most prominent of many public utterances. In the first scene, Marullus rebukes the plebeians for their disloyalty to Pompey, and for the moment dissuades them from idolizing Caesar. Decius Brutus changes Caesar's presumably unalterable mind about staying home on the ides of March (2.2). Caesar lectures the Senate on the virtues of constancy. Before Philippi, the contending armies clash with verbal taunts. Octavius ends the play with a tribute to the dead Brutus. In less public scenes, as well, oratory serves to win Brutus over to the conspirators, to urge unavailingly that Brutus confide in his wife, or to warn the unheeding Caesar of his danger. The decline of the conspirators' cause is reflected in their descent from rational discourse to private bickering (4.3). The play gives us a range of rhetorical styles, from the deliberative (having to do with careful consideration of choices) to the forensic (analogous to pleading at law, maintaining one side or the other of a given question), to the epideictic (for display, as in set orations). The imagery, suitably public and rhetorical in its function, is of a fixed star in the firmament, a Colossus bestriding the petty world of men, a tide of fortune in the affairs of men, a statue spouting fountains of blood. The city of Rome is a vivid presence in the play, conveyed at times through Elizabethan anachronisms such as striking clocks, sweaty nightcaps, "towers and windows, yea, . . . chimney tops" (1.1.39), but in an eclectic fusion of native and classical traditions wherein anachronisms become functionally purposeful. Style affords us one more way of considering *Julius Caesar* as a Janus play looking back to Shakespeare's history plays and forward to his tragedies.

A structural pattern to be found in *Julius Caesar* is the replicating action of rise and fall by which the great men of ancient Rome succeed one another. The process antedates the play itself, for Pompey's faded glory mentioned in Act 1 is a reminder—or should be a reminder—that any person's rise to fortune lasts but a day. We behold Caesar at the point of his greatest triumph and his imminent decline to death. "O mighty Caesar! Dost thou lie so low?" asks Antony when he sees the prostrate body of the once most powerful man alive. "Are all thy conquests, glories, triumphs, spoils, / Shrunk to this little measure?" (3.1.150–152). Brutus and Cassius step forward into prominence only to be supplanted by Antony and Octavius. Antony is unaware, though presumably the audience is aware, that Antony is to fall at the hands of Octavius. The process of incessant change, reinforced by such metaphors as the tide in the affairs of men (already noted), offering its mocking comment on Caesar's self-comparison to the fixed northern star, is not simply a meaningless descent on the grand staircase of history, for Octavius' *Pax Romana* lies at the end of the cycle from republic to empire. Still, that resting place is beyond the conclusion of this open-ended play. What we see here again and again is a human blindness to history through which a succession of protagonists repeat one another's errors without intending to do so. Cassius, like Caesar, goes to his death in the face of unpropitious omens that he now partly believes true. The eagles that accompanied Cassius and his army to Philippi desert him as the moment of battle approaches. These omens suggest a balance between character and fate, for, though the leaders of Rome have one by one fallen through their own acts and choices, they have also, it seems, fulfilled a prearranged destiny. Brutus, confronted by the Ghost of Caesar and assured that he will see this spirit of Caesar at Philippi, answers resolutely, "Why, I will see thee at Philippi, then" (4.3.288). Defeated in battle as he sensed he would be, Brutus unwillingly takes his life in disregard of the stoic creed that has governed the conduct of his entire life. Cassius dies on his birthday. *Sic transit gloria mundi.*

Julius Caesar
in Performance

As a play about political conflict, *Julius Caesar* has lent itself again and again to political interpretation. No reports have survived from Shakespeare's own day to let us know what his contemporaries thought of the play politically (though it seems to have been popular, and some inferences may be drawn from the fact that the play was performed before Charles I in 1637 and again the following year), but to the Restoration and eighteenth century the play clearly was a ringing defense of republicanism and freedom versus the tyranny of Caesar. Thomas Betterton until 1707, Barton Booth until 1728, and James Quin until 1751 played Brutus as the eloquent and noble soul of liberty. The play was predominantly Brutus'; he was, as the actor and dramatist Colley Cibber wrote, a "philosopher and the hero," and the play's "lesson" was a warning against the kind of autocratic rule from which England had struggled to free herself in the seventeenth century.

Performance of the play was intended to stir feelings of national pride and love of liberty. Oratorical skill in delivering impassioned noble sentiments mattered more than nuance of character. Brutus' death became, with some added lines, one last noble sacrifice made for freedom, a protest against "poor slavish Rome" in the grip of Caesarism. Mark Antony, as acted by Edward Kynaston, Robert Wilks, and William Milward, was either cast in Brutus' shadow or made to appear to be, like Brutus, another defender of freedom. Other textual modifications reduced Julius Caesar to the tyrant that audiences expected. Minor figures were cleared away, such as Cinna the Poet (3.3) and the poet of Act 4, scene 3; Artemidorus and the Soothsayer were often merged into one, and Casca's role was usually expanded to include the lines of Marullus in Act 1, scene 1, and Titinius later in the play. The play's supposed improprieties were purified; for example, Portia was reported to have wounded herself in the arm instead of her thigh.

Between 1812 and his retirement in 1817, John Philip

Kemble had great success with the play at the Theatre Royal, Covent Garden, performing it along similar lines, simplifying the plot and intensifying the idealization of Brutus through a Romantic interest in Roman grandeur. Kemble added to the usual excisions still another cut: the disillusioning scene (4.1) in which Antony consents with Octavius to the proscribing of a number of their political enemies, even close relations. Costuming, always at least partly Roman even in Shakespeare's day (though blended at that time with anachronistic touches of contemporary dress), in the nineteenth century became a matter of scrupulous archaeological restoration. Kemble took inordinate trouble with stage picture, grouping large numbers of supernumeraries in front of painted scenery inspired by Joshua Reynolds and the Royal Academy, where pictorial interest in the inspiring antiquities of Rome had wide currency. Kemble's Brutus was more than ever the lofty patriot, while Antony, played by Kemble's brother Charles, avenged the death of Caesar from the best of motives. The cutting of the text aimed at symmetry between opposing forces and simplification of character. Kemble's version gave its spectators what they wanted, and thereafter in the nineteenth century *Julius Caesar* was seldom absent from the repertory.

The play appeared regularly onstage in the United States as well, where it no doubt appealed to the new republic's political sympathies. Lewis Hallam produced the play several times in the late eighteenth century, acting Brutus, most notably at New York's John Street Theatre in 1794. In the early nineteenth century, Thomas Abthorpe Cooper drew record crowds with his productions at the Park Theatre in New York and on tour, including a performance at Charleston, South Carolina, in 1819 attended by President Monroe.

Though critics praised Cooper's acting, they did occasionally complain, as did a Boston critic in 1818, that he had "not introduced into his performance all the stage business which has been recently invented in England." Two developments were increasingly evident on the British stage in the years after Kemble: the use of expensive realistic sets and costuming, and a political shift toward the viewpoint of the people of Rome. Nineteenth-century productions were often so lavish in their zeal for naturalistic stage pictures that the scenery determined what was to remain in the text. William Charles Macready, at Covent Garden in 1838 and five years later at the Theatre Royal, Drury Lane, bestowed on the play a passion for the details of historical setting that had begun with Kemble. Macready used painted shutters with accurate representations of Roman scenes, and employed over a hundred supernumeraries in order to give material substance to the participation of Rome's citizenry. Edwin Booth provided sets of even greater splendor for his production in New York at Booth's Theatre in 1871. The assassination of Caesar took place in a replica of the Roman Senate House based on a painting by Gérôme, with overarching paneled ceilings, rows of statuary, classical columns, banks of seats for the senators, and a seat of state for the ill-fated Caesar. Herbert Beerbohm Tree's production in 1898 at Her Majesty's Theatre was a culmination of the grand style, a spectacular three-act version rearranged to highlight the scenery and Tree himself. The middle act, given over entirely to the Forum scene, focused on Antony (played by Tree) as he spoke to an immense crowd, with handsome facades and details of the ancient Roman Forum in the background. In each act Tree was allowed to have the tableau curtain chiefly to himself, and his role was ennobled by the cutting of those scenes and speeches not to Antony's credit.

A shift in political interest manifested itself in the attention newly paid to characters other than Brutus. Macready sometimes chose to play not Brutus but Cassius, who fascinated Macready with his energy, rancorous ambition, and keen intellect. Even when Macready took the more usual role for the lead actor, that of Brutus, he brought out a more complex figure than had been seen heretofore, abhorring tyranny still, of course, but tender, gentle, self-subdued. Samuel Phelps also played both Cassius and Brutus, the former in Macready's productions of 1838 and 1843 and the latter chiefly at the Sadler's Wells Theatre between 1846 and 1862. (Brutus was in fact his farewell role at Sadler's Wells on November 6, 1862.) Edwin Booth played Brutus in his spectacular production of 1871, but he also later played both Cassius and Antony, gaining thereby an insight into the contending sides in the political struggle for Rome. The Duke

of Saxe-Meiningen's company, playing in German at Drury
Lane in 1881, presented a startling, well-orchestrated crowd
scene in which the spirit of a disturbing political movement appeared much larger than Brutus or Caesar as in-
dividuals. The populace of Rome was at last gaining in
importance onstage.

A major trend of twentieth-century interpretation has
been to ironize the play, to see it as a portrait of conflict in
which all politicians are fundamentally alike and in which
the chief causes for which people strive are illusory. At its
best, as in an Old Vic production in 1932 with Ralph Rich-
ardson as Brutus and Robert Speaight as Cassius, and
another at Stratford-upon-Avon in 1950 directed by Anthony
Quayle and Michael Langham, this ironic distancing has
led to a balanced view of political struggle, one in which
Brutus and Caesar are indeed often alike; the parallel and
adjoining scenes 1 and 2 in the second act offer directors
ample opportunity to point up similarities as Brutus and
then Caesar receive the conspirators at their houses and
disregard the advice of their wives. Strong acting on the
part of John Gielgud (Cassius) and Andrew Cruickshank
(Caesar) in 1950 provided a healthy counterpart to the usual
dominance of Brutus and Antony (played on this occasion
by Harry Andrews and Anthony Quayle), resulting in an im-
partial and wryly compassionate wholeness of view. The
set, as in most other twentieth-century productions, es-
chewed the heavy realistic scenery of the nineteenth century in favor of a sparse symbolism. Joseph Mankiewicz's
film version of *Julius Caesar* (1953), embarrassingly cast
with Marlon Brando as Antony and James Mason as a be-
mused and irritatedly indecisive Brutus, but with Gielgud
once again as Cassius, Louis Calhern as Caesar, and Deb-
orah Kerr as Portia, sought at least a kind of symmetry in
its star casting that allowed the play to speak for itself. Joseph Papp's 1962 swift-paced production at the Heckscher
Theater in New York used Thea Neu's simple, imaginative
set and strong performances from its principal actors to
keep the play's political energies in provocative balance.
Terry Hands's production at Stratford-upon-Avon in 1987
found a more telling equilibrium in subordinating the political opposition between Caesar and Brutus to an emphasis

upon what Hands called the debilitating "effects of power in a male dominated world."

Inevitably, in some productions a darker view of political machination has taken a more ideologically determined shape when the director has deliberately chosen to unbalance the play's symmetries and aim at a partisan effect. Orson Welles, in a production subtitled *Death of a Dictator* (New York, Mercury Theater, 1937), drew an analogy between Caesar and Benito Mussolini. The killing of Cinna the Poet demonstrated the pathetic vulnerability of innocence in the face of the inhuman brutality of an angry mob. Caesar was a caricature of the modern dictator, with thrust-out chin and Fascist uniform; Antony was a rabble-rouser of ominous rhetorical ability. Brutus was a thoughtful man, able to inspire his followers with dedication but ultimately victimized by his own idealism, since he was unable to do more than release the forces of chaos that mocked his dream of freedom from tyranny. Welles added to the contemporary relevance with technical aspects of production: he employed the episodic format of a film script, using lighting and sound effects rather than scenery changes to move rapidly from one scene to another. Dallas Bower, directing the play for BBC television in July of 1938, similarly exploited the play's relevance to the contemporary political situation, prophetically ending his modern-dress version with the sound of bombers overhead. Late in the autumn of 1939, with Europe now at war, Henry Cass, at London's Embassy Theatre, polemically set the play in Fascist Europe, to the point of dressing Antony in an SS uniform and providing field telephones for the commanding officers during the battle in Act 5.

Since World War II, the modern world has not failed to provide new targets for this kind of pointed political comment. Brewster Mason, playing Caesar with haughty demeanor and humorless authority in John Barton's Royal Shakespeare Company production of 1968, reminded audiences of General Charles de Gaulle. In 1969 at the Guthrie Theater in Minneapolis, Edward Payson Call used sets and costumes to evoke the atmosphere of a Latin American dictatorship. The political frame of reference can also be meaningful and contemporary when it is less specific, as at

Stratford-upon-Avon in 1972, when Trevor Nunn, Evan Smith, and Buzz Goodbody generalized the portrait of Caesarism to embrace all political oppression. A colossal statue of Caesar, onstage throughout much of the play subsequent to the assassination, towered impassively above those who still struggled against their destiny, and presided with grim satisfaction over the demise of those who had conspired against him. In 1977 at London's National Theatre, the Caesar of John Gielgud similarly remained wordlessly and ominously onstage in the wake of his murder, and at Philippi four "Caesars" surrounded Brutus to indicate the impossibility of escape from Caesarism in human history.

Even without the explicit context of fascism, then, the play in the twentieth century has retained its political relevance. Modern productions have generally seen Caesar as the embodiment of tyranny but have been unwilling to see Brutus as a viable alternative. A world grown skeptical of politics and politicians has tended to find neither Brutus nor Caesar a compelling hero; if Caesar is arrogant, Brutus is self-deceived. Modern productions have accordingly traced the dispiriting cycle by which revolution generates counterrevolution and tyranny gives way to new tyranny. Such a vision of the play no doubt tells us more about our politics than about Shakespeare's, but it testifies also to the play's remarkable ability to elicit responses as complex as the ceaseless struggle for power the play depicts.

The Playhouse

This early copy of a drawing by Johannes de Witt of the Swan Theatre in London (c. 1596), made by his friend Arend van Buchell, is the only surviving contemporary sketch of the interior of a public theater in the 1590s.

From other contemporary evidence, including the stage directions and dialogue of Elizabethan plays, we can surmise that the various public theaters where Shakespeare's plays were produced (the Theatre, the Curtain, the Globe) resembled the Swan in many important particulars, though there must have been some variations as well. The public playhouses were essentially round, or polygonal, and open to the sky, forming an acting arena approximately 70 feet in diameter; they did not have a large curtain with which to open and close a scene, such as we see today in opera and some traditional theater. A platform measuring approximately 43 feet across and 27 feet deep, referred to in the de Witt drawing as the *proscaenium*, projected into the yard, *planities sive arena*. The roof, *tectum*, above the stage and supported by two pillars, could contain machinery for ascents and descents, as were required in several of Shakespeare's late plays. Above this roof was a hut, shown in the drawing with a flag flying atop it and a trumpeter at its door announcing the performance of a play. The underside of the stage roof, called the heavens, was usually richly decorated with symbolic figures of the sun, the moon, and the constellations. The platform stage stood at a height of 5½ feet or so above the yard, providing room under the stage for underworldly effects. A trapdoor, which is not visible in this drawing, gave access to the space below.

The structure at the back of the platform (labeled *mimorum aedes*), known as the tiring-house because it was the actors' attiring (dressing) space, featured at least two doors, as shown here. Some theaters seem to have also had a discovery space, or curtained recessed alcove, perhaps between the two doors—in which Falstaff could have hidden from the sheriff (*1 Henry IV*, 2.4) or Polonius could have eavesdropped on Hamlet and his mother (*Hamlet*, 3.4). This discovery space probably gave the actors a means of access to and from the tiring-house. Curtains may also have been hung in front of the stage doors on occasion. The de Witt drawing shows a gallery above the doors that extends across the back and evidently contains spectators. On occasions when action "above" demanded the use of this space, as when Juliet appears at her "window" (*Romeo and Juliet*, 2.2 and 3.5), the gallery seems to have been used by the actors, but large scenes there were impractical.

The three-tiered auditorium is perhaps best described by Thomas Platter, a visitor to London in 1599 who saw on that occasion Shakespeare's *Julius Caesar* performed at the Globe:

The playhouses are so constructed that they play on a raised platform, so that everyone has a good view. There are different galleries and places [*orchestra, sedilia, porticus*], however, where the seating is better and more comfortable and therefore more expensive. For whoever cares to stand below only pays one English penny, but if he wishes to sit, he enters by another door [*ingressus*] and pays another penny, while if he desires to sit in the most comfortable seats, which are cushioned, where he not only sees everything well but can also be seen, then he pays yet another English penny at another door. And during the performance food and drink are carried round the audience, so that for what one cares to pay one may also have refreshment.

Scenery was not used, though the theater building itself was handsome enough to invoke a feeling of order and hierarchy that lent itself to the splendor and pageantry onstage. Portable properties, such as thrones, stools, tables, and beds, could be carried or thrust on as needed. In the scene pictured here by de Witt, a lady on a bench, attended perhaps by her waiting-gentlewoman, receives the address of a male figure. If Shakespeare had written *Twelfth Night* by 1596 for performance at the Swan, we could imagine Malvolio appearing like this as he bows before the Countess Olivia and her gentlewoman, Maria.

JULIUS CAESAR

PINDARUS, *Cassius' servant*
LUCIUS,
STRATO, } *Brutus' servants*
Caesar's SERVANT
Antony's SERVANT
Octavius' SERVANT

CARPENTER
COBBLER
Five PLEBEIANS
Three SOLDIERS *in Brutus' army*
Two SOLDIERS *in Antony's army*
MESSENGER

GHOST *of Caesar*

Senators, Plebeians, Officers, Soldiers, and Attendants

SCENE: *Rome; the neighborhood of Sardis; the neighborhood of Philippi*]

1.1 *Enter Flavius, Marullus, and certain commoners over the stage.*

FLAVIUS
Hence! Home, you idle creatures, get you home!
Is this a holiday? What, know you not,
Being mechanical, you ought not walk   3
Upon a laboring day without the sign   4
Of your profession? Speak, what trade art thou?

CARPENTER Why, sir, a carpenter.

MARULLUS
Where is thy leather apron and thy rule?
What dost thou with thy best apparel on?
You, sir, what trade are you?

COBBLER Truly, sir, in respect of a fine workman, I am 10
but, as you would say, a cobbler.   11

MARULLUS
But what trade art thou? Answer me directly.

COBBLER A trade, sir, that I hope I may use with a safe
conscience, which is indeed, sir, a mender of bad soles. 14

FLAVIUS
What trade, thou knave? Thou naughty knave, what
trade?   15

COBBLER Nay, I beseech you, sir, be not out with me.   16
Yet if you be out, sir, I can mend you.   17

MARULLUS
What mean'st thou by that? Mend me, thou saucy fellow?

COBBLER Why, sir, cobble you.   19

FLAVIUS Thou art a cobbler, art thou?

COBBLER Truly, sir, all that I live by is with the awl. I
meddle with no tradesman's matters nor women's   22
matters, but withal I am indeed, sir, a surgeon to old   23

1.1. Location: Rome. A street.
3 mechanical of the class of artisans **4 sign** garb and implements
10 in . . . workman (1) as far as skilled work is concerned (2) compared
with a skilled workman **11 cobbler** (1) one who works with shoes
(2) bungler **14 soles** (with pun on *souls*) **15 naughty** good-for-
nothing **16–17 out** (1) out of temper (2) having worn-out soles
17 mend (1) reform (2) repair **19 cobble** (The meaning "to pelt with
stones" suggests itself here, though perhaps not in general use until
later in the seventeenth century.) **22–23 meddle, women's matters**
(with sexual suggestion) **23 withal** yet (with pun on *with awl*)

shoes. When they are in great danger, I recover them.   24
As proper men as ever trod upon neat's leather have   25
gone upon my handiwork.   26

FLAVIUS

But wherefore art not in thy shop today?
Why dost thou lead these men about the streets?

COBBLER   Truly, sir, to wear out their shoes, to get myself into more work. But indeed, sir, we make holiday
to see Caesar and to rejoice in his triumph.   31

MARULLUS

Wherefore rejoice? What conquest brings he home?
What tributaries follow him to Rome   33
To grace in captive bonds his chariot wheels?
You blocks, you stones, you worse than senseless things! 35
O you hard hearts, you cruel men of Rome,
Knew you not Pompey? Many a time and oft   37
Have you climbed up to walls and battlements,   38
To towers and windows, yea, to chimney tops,   39
Your infants in your arms, and there have sat
The livelong day, with patient expectation,
To see great Pompey pass the streets of Rome.   42
And when you saw his chariot but appear,
Have you not made an universal shout,
That Tiber trembled underneath her banks   45
To hear the replication of your sounds   46
Made in her concave shores?
And do you now put on your best attire?
And do you now cull out a holiday?   49
And do you now strew flowers in his way
That comes in triumph over Pompey's blood?   51
Begone!

24 recover (1) resole (2) cure   **25 proper** handsome.   **as . . . leather** as
ever wore shoes. (Proverbial.)   **neat's leather** cowhide   **26 gone** walked
31 triumph triumphal procession. (Caesar had overthrown the sons of
Pompey in Spain at the Battle of Munda, March 17, 45 B.C. The triumph
was held that October.)   **33 tributaries** captives who will pay ransom
(tribute)   **35 senseless** insensible like stone (hence, stupid)   **37 Pompey**
(Caesar had overthrown the great soldier and onetime triumvir at the
Battle of Pharsalus in 48 B.C., and Pompey fled to Egypt where he was
murdered.)   **38–39 battlements . . . chimney tops** (The details are
appropriate to an Elizabethan city or town.)   **42 great** (Alludes to
Pompey's epithet, *Magnus*, great.)   **pass** pass through   **45 Tiber** the
Tiber River   **46 replication** echo   **49 cull out** select, pick out
51 Pompey's blood (1) Pompey's offspring (2) the blood of the Pompeys

Run to your houses, fall upon your knees,
Pray to the gods to intermit the plague   54
That needs must light on this ingratitude.   ˜55

FLAVIUS

Go, go, good countrymen, and for this fault
Assemble all the poor men of your sort;   57
Draw them to Tiber banks, and weep your tears
Into the channel, till the lowest stream
Do kiss the most exalted shores of all.   60
                                        Exeunt all the commoners.
See whe'er their basest mettle be not moved.   61
They vanish tongue-tied in their guiltiness.
Go you down that way towards the Capitol;
This way will I. Disrobe the images   64
If you do find them decked with ceremonies.   65

MARULLUS   May we do so?
You know it is the Feast of Lupercal.   67

FLAVIUS

It is no matter. Let no images
Be hung with Caesar's trophies. I'll about   69
And drive away the vulgar from the streets;   70
So do you too, where you perceive them thick.
These growing feathers plucked from Caesar's wing
Will make him fly an ordinary pitch,   73
Who else would soar above the view of men   74
And keep us all in servile fearfulness.   *Exeunt.*

❖

54 intermit withhold   **55 needs must** must necessarily   **57 sort** rank
60 kiss i.e., touch.   **most exalted shores** highest banks   **61 See . . . moved**
see how even their ignoble natures can be appealed to.   **whe'er**
whether.   **mettle** (1) temperament (2) substance, *metal*. (*Metal* and *mettle*
are variants of the same word. A *base metal* is one that is easily changed
or *moved*, unlike gold; compare 1.2.309.)   **64 images** statues (of Caesar in
royal regalia, set up by his followers)   **65 ceremonies** ceremonial trap-
pings of state   **67 Feast of Lupercal** a feast of purification (*Februa*,
whence *February*) in honor of Pan, celebrated from ancient times in Rome
on February 15 of each year. (Historically, this celebration came some
months after Caesar's triumph in October of 45 B.C. The celebrants,
called *Luperci*, raced around the Palatine Hill and the Circus carrying
thongs of goatskin with which they struck those who came in their way.
Women so lashed were supposed to be cured of barrenness; hence Caesar's wish that Antony would strike Calpurnia, 1.2.6–8.)   **69 about** go
about   **70 vulgar** commoners, plebeians   **73 pitch** highest point in flight.
(A term from falconry.)   **74 else** otherwise

1.2   *Enter Caesar, Antony for the course, Calpurnia,*
      Portia, Decius, Cicero, Brutus, Cassius, Casca, a
      Soothsayer; after them, Marullus and Flavius;
      [citizens following].

CAESAR
  Calpurnia!
CASCA   Peace, ho! Caesar speaks.
CAESAR   Calpurnia!
CALPURNIA   Here, my lord.
CAESAR
  Stand you directly in Antonius' way
  When he doth run his course. Antonius!
ANTONY   Caesar, my lord?
CAESAR
  Forget not, in your speed, Antonius,
  To touch Calpurnia; for our elders say
  The barren, touchèd in this holy chase,
  Shake off their sterile curse.
ANTONY   I shall remember.   9
  When Caesar says "Do this," it is performed.
CAESAR
  Set on, and leave no ceremony out.   [*Flourish.*]   11
SOOTHSAYER   Caesar!
CAESAR   Ha? Who calls?
CASCA
  Bid every noise be still. Peace yet again!
                         [*The music ceases.*]
CAESAR
  Who is it in the press that calls on me?   15
  I hear a tongue shriller than all the music
  Cry "Caesar!" Speak. Caesar is turned to hear.
SOOTHSAYER
  Beware the ides of March.
CAESAR   What man is that?   18
BRUTUS
  A soothsayer bids you beware the ides of March.

1.2. Location: A public place or street, perhaps as in the previous scene.
s.d. for the course i.e., stripped for the race, carrying a goatskin
thong   **9 sterile curse** curse of sterility   **11 Set on** proceed   **15 press**
throng   **18 ides of March** March 15

CAESAR
    Set him before me. Let me see his face.
CASSIUS
    Fellow, come from the throng. [*The Soothsayer comes*
      forward.] Look upon Caesar.
CAESAR
    What sayst thou to me now? Speak once again.
SOOTHSAYER   Beware the ides of March.
CAESAR
    He is a dreamer. Let us leave him. Pass.   24
         Sennet. Exeunt. Manent Brutus and Cassius.
CASSIUS
    Will you go see the order of the course?   25
BRUTUS   Not I.
CASSIUS   I pray you, do.
BRUTUS
    I am not gamesome. I do lack some part   28
    Of that quick spirit that is in Antony.   29
    Let me not hinder, Cassius, your desires;
    I'll leave you.
CASSIUS
    Brutus, I do observe you now of late.
    I have not from your eyes that gentleness
    And show of love as I was wont to have.   34
    You bear too stubborn and too strange a hand   35
    Over your friend that loves you.
BRUTUS   Cassius,
    Be not deceived. If I have veiled my look,   37
    I turn the trouble of my countenance
    Merely upon myself. Vexèd I am   39
    Of late with passions of some difference,   40
    Conceptions only proper to myself,   41
    Which give some soil, perhaps, to my behaviors. 42
    But let not therefore my good friends be grieved—
    Among which number, Cassius, be you one—

24 s.d. Sennet trumpet call signaling the arrival or departure of a
dignitary. **Manent** they remain onstage **25 order of the course** ritual
of the race **28 gamesome** fond of sports, merry **29 quick spirit**
liveliness, responsiveness **34 wont** accustomed **35 stubborn** rough.
(The metaphor is from horsemanship.) **strange** unfriendly **37 veiled
my look** i.e., been introverted, seemed less friendly **39 Merely** entirely **40 of some difference** conflicting **41 only proper to** relating
only to **42 soil** blemish

Nor construe any further my neglect   45
Than that poor Brutus, with himself at war,
Forgets the shows of love to other men.
CASSIUS
Then, Brutus, I have much mistook your passion,
By means whereof this breast of mine hath buried   49
Thoughts of great value, worthy cogitations.   50
Tell me, good Brutus, can you see your face?
BRUTUS
No, Cassius, for the eye sees not itself
But by reflection, by some other things.
CASSIUS   'Tis just.   54
And it is very much lamented, Brutus,
That you have no such mirrors as will turn
Your hidden worthiness into your eye,
That you might see your shadow. I have heard   58
Where many of the best respect in Rome,   59
Except immortal Caesar, speaking of Brutus
And groaning underneath this age's yoke,
Have wished that noble Brutus had his eyes.   62
BRUTUS
Into what dangers would you lead me, Cassius,
That you would have me seek into myself
For that which is not in me?
CASSIUS
Therefore, good Brutus, be prepared to hear;
And since you know you cannot see yourself
So well as by reflection, I, your glass,   68
Will modestly discover to yourself   69
That of yourself which you yet know not of.
And be not jealous on me, gentle Brutus.   71
Were I a common laughter, or did use   72
To stale with ordinary oaths my love   73

45 construe interpret. further otherwise   49–50 By . . . value i.e.,
because of which misunderstanding (my assuming you were displeased
with me) I have kept to myself important thoughts   54 just true
58 shadow image, reflection   59 best respect highest repute and station   62 had his eyes (1) could see things from the perspective of Caesar's critics, or (2) could see better with his own eyes   68 glass
mirror   69 modestly discover reveal without exaggeration   71 jealous
on suspicious of. gentle noble   72 laughter laughingstock. did use
were accustomed   73 stale cheapen, make common. ordinary
(1) commonplace (2) customary (3) tavern

To every new protester; if you know 74
That I do fawn on men and hug them hard
And after scandal them, or if you know 76
That I profess myself in banqueting 77
To all the rout, then hold me dangerous. 78

Flourish, and shout.

BRUTUS
What means this shouting? I do fear the people
Choose Caesar for their king.

CASSIUS   Ay, do you fear it?
Then must I think you would not have it so.

BRUTUS
I would not, Cassius, yet I love him well.
But wherefore do you hold me here so long?
What is it that you would impart to me?
If it be aught toward the general good,
Set honor in one eye and death i' th' other
And I will look on both indifferently; 87
For let the gods so speed me as I love 88
The name of honor more than I fear death.

CASSIUS
I know that virtue to be in you, Brutus,
As well as I do know your outward favor. 91
Well, honor is the subject of my story.
I cannot tell what you and other men
Think of this life; but, for my single self,
I had as lief not be as live to be 95
In awe of such a thing as I myself. 96
I was born free as Caesar, so were you;
We both have fed as well, and we can both
Endure the winter's cold as well as he.
For once, upon a raw and gusty day,
The troubled Tiber chafing with her shores, 101
Caesar said to me, "Dar'st thou, Cassius, now
Leap in with me into this angry flood
And swim to yonder point?" Upon the word,

74 protester i.e., one who protests or declares friendship   **76 scandal**
slander   **77 profess myself** make declarations of friendship   **78 rout**
mob   **87 indifferently** impartially   **88 speed me** make me prosper
91 favor appearance   **95 as lief not be** just as soon not exist   **96 such**
. . . **myself** i.e., a fellow mortal   **101 chafing with** raging against

Accoutered as I was, I plungèd in   105
And bade him follow; so indeed he did.
The torrent roared, and we did buffet it
With lusty sinews, throwing it aside
And stemming it with hearts of controversy.   109
But ere we could arrive the point proposed,   110
Caesar cried, "Help me, Cassius, or I sink!"
Ay, as Aeneas, our great ancestor,   112
Did from the flames of Troy upon his shoulder
The old Anchises bear, so from the waves of Tiber
Did I the tirèd Caesar. And this man
Is now become a god, and Cassius is
A wretched creature and must bend his body   117
If Caesar carelessly but nod on him.
He had a fever when he was in Spain,
And when the fit was on him I did mark   120
How he did shake. 'Tis true, this god did shake.
His coward lips did from their color fly,   122
And that same eye whose bend doth awe the world 123
Did lose his luster. I did hear him groan.   124
Ay, and that tongue of his that bade the Romans
Mark him and write his speeches in their books,
Alas, it cried, "Give me some drink, Titinius,"
As a sick girl. Ye gods, it doth amaze me
A man of such a feeble temper should   129
So get the start of the majestic world   130
And bear the palm alone.   *Shout. Flourish.* 131
BRUTUS   Another general shout?
I do believe that these applauses are
For some new honors that are heaped on Caesar.
CASSIUS
Why, man, he doth bestride the narrow world   135

---

105 Accoutered fully armed, dressed   **109 stemming** making headway
against.   **hearts of controversy** hearts fired up by rivalry   **110 arrive**
arrive at   **112 Aeneas** hero of Virgil's *Aeneid*, the legendary founder of
Rome (hence *our great ancestor*), who bore his aged father Anchises out
of burning Troy as it was falling to the Greeks   **117 bend his body**
bow   **120 mark** notice   **122 color** (1) i.e., normal healthy hue (2) military colors, flag. (The lips are personified as deserters.)   **123 bend**
glance, gaze   **124 his** its   **129 temper** constitution   **130 get the start of**
outstrip   **131 palm** victor's prize   **135 bestride** straddle

Like a Colossus, and we petty men   136
Walk under his huge legs and peep about
To find ourselves dishonorable graves.   138
Men at some time are masters of their fates.
The fault, dear Brutus, is not in our stars,
But in ourselves, that we are underlings.
"Brutus" and "Caesar." What should be in that
  "Caesar"?
Why should that name be sounded more than yours?
Write them together, yours is as fair a name;
Sound them, it doth become the mouth as well;
Weigh them, it is as heavy; conjure with 'em,
"Brutus" will start a spirit as soon as "Caesar."   147
Now, in the names of all the gods at once,
Upon what meat doth this our Caesar feed   149
That he is grown so great? Age, thou art shamed!
Rome, thou hast lost the breed of noble bloods!
When went there by an age since the great flood   152
But it was famed with more than with one man?   153
When could they say, till now, that talked of Rome,
That her wide walks encompassed but one man?
Now is it Rome indeed, and room enough,   156
When there is in it but one only man.
O, you and I have heard our fathers say
There was a Brutus once that would have brooked   159
Th' eternal devil to keep his state in Rome   160
As easily as a king.   161

BRUTUS
That you do love me, I am nothing jealous.   162
What you would work me to, I have some aim.   163

---

136 Colossus (A 100-foot-high bronze statue of Helios, the sun god, one
of the seven wonders of the ancient world, was commonly supposed to
have stood astride the entrance to the harbor of Rhodes.)
138 dishonorable graves the ignoble deaths of slaves   **147 start** raise
149 meat food   **152 flood** i.e., the classical analogue of Noah's flood,
one in which all humanity was destroyed except for Deucalion and his
wife Pyrrha   **153 famed with** famous for   **156 Rome, room** (Pro-
nounced alike.)   **159 Brutus** i.e., Lucius Junius Brutus, who expelled
the Tarquins and founded the Roman republic (c. 509 B.C.).   **brooked**
tolerated   **160 keep his state** i.e., set up his throne   **161 As . . . king** as
readily as he would tolerate a king   **162 nothing jealous** not at all
doubtful   **163 work** persuade.   **aim** inkling and intention

How I have thought of this and of these times
I shall recount hereafter. For this present,   165
I would not, so with love I might entreat you,   166
Be any further moved. What you have said   167
I will consider; what you have to say
I will with patience hear, and find a time
Both meet to hear and answer such high things.   170
Till then, my noble friend, chew upon this:
Brutus had rather be a villager
Than to repute himself a son of Rome
Under these hard conditions as this time
Is like to lay upon us.
CASSIUS I am glad that my weak words
Have struck but thus much show of fire from Brutus.

    Enter Caesar and his train.

BRUTUS
The games are done and Caesar is returning.
CASSIUS
As they pass by, pluck Casca by the sleeve,
And he will, after his sour fashion, tell you
What hath proceeded worthy note today.   181
BRUTUS
I will do so. But look you, Cassius,
The angry spot doth glow on Caesar's brow,
And all the rest look like a chidden train.   184
Calpurnia's cheek is pale, and Cicero
Looks with such ferret and such fiery eyes   186
As we have seen him in the Capitol,
Being crossed in conference by some senators.   188
CASSIUS
Casca will tell us what the matter is.
CAESAR Antonius!
ANTONY Caesar?
CAESAR
Let me have men about me that are fat,

165 present present moment **166 so . . . you** if I might entreat you in
the name of friendship **167 moved** urged **170 meet** fitting
181 worthy note worthy of notice **184 chidden** scolded, rebuked. **train**
retinue **186 ferret** ferretlike, i.e., small and red **188 crossed in conference** opposed in debate

Sleek-headed men, and such as sleep o' nights.
Yond Cassius has a lean and hungry look.
He thinks too much. Such men are dangerous.

ANTONY

Fear him not, Caesar, he's not dangerous.
He is a noble Roman, and well given.   197

CAESAR

Would he were fatter! But I fear him not.
Yet if my name were liable to fear,
I do not know the man I should avoid
So soon as that spare Cassius. He reads much,
He is a great observer, and he looks
Quite through the deeds of men. He loves no plays,   203
As thou dost, Antony; he hears no music.   204
Seldom he smiles, and smiles in such a sort   205
As if he mocked himself and scorned his spirit
That could be moved to smile at anything.
Such men as he be never at heart's ease
Whiles they behold a greater than themselves,
And therefore are they very dangerous.
I rather tell thee what is to be feared
Than what I fear, for always I am Caesar.
Come on my right hand, for this ear is deaf,
And tell me truly what thou think'st of him.
                    Sennet. Exeunt Caesar and his train. [Casca
                          remains with Brutus and Cassius.]

CASCA   You pulled me by the cloak. Would you speak   215
with me?

BRUTUS

Ay, Casca. Tell us what hath chanced today,   217
That Caesar looks so sad.   218

CASCA   Why, you were with him, were you not?

BRUTUS

I should not then ask Casca what had chanced.

CASCA   Why, there was a crown offered him; and, being
offered him, he put it by with the back of his hand,   222
thus, and then the people fell a-shouting.

197 given disposed   **203 through** i.e., into the motives of   **204 hears no music** (Regarded as a sign of a morose and treacherous character.)   **205 sort**
manner   **215 cloak** (Elizabethan costume; see also *sleeve*, l. 179, and *doublet*,
l. 265)   **217 chanced** happened   **218 sad** serious   **222 by** aside

BRUTUS What was the second noise for?

CASCA Why, for that too.

CASSIUS
They shouted thrice. What was the last cry for?

CASCA Why, for that too.

BRUTUS Was the crown offered him thrice?

CASCA Ay, marry, was 't, and he put it by thrice, every   229
time gentler than other, and at every putting-by mine
honest neighbors shouted.   231

CASSIUS Who offered him the crown?

CASCA Why, Antony.

BRUTUS
Tell us the manner of it, gentle Casca.   234

CASCA I can as well be hanged as tell the manner of it.
It was mere foolery; I did not mark it. I saw Mark Antony offer him a crown—yet 'twas not a crown neither, 'twas one of these coronets—and, as I told you,   238
he put it by once; but for all that, to my thinking, he
would fain have had it. Then he offered it to him again;   240
then he put it by again; but to my thinking he was
very loath to lay his fingers off it. And then he offered
it the third time. He put it the third time by, and still   243
as he refused it the rabblement hooted and clapped   244
their chapped hands, and threw up their sweaty night-   245
caps, and uttered such a deal of stinking breath be-   246
cause Caesar refused the crown that it had almost
choked Caesar, for he swooned and fell down at it.
And for mine own part I durst not laugh for fear of
opening my lips and receiving the bad air.

CASSIUS
But soft, I pray you. What, did Caesar swoon?   251

CASCA He fell down in the marketplace, and foamed at
mouth, and was speechless.

BRUTUS
'Tis very like. He hath the falling sickness.   254

---

229 marry i.e., indeed. (Originally, "by the Virgin Mary.")   **231 honest**
worthy. (Said contemptuously.)   **234 gentle** noble   **238 coronets** chap-
lets, garlands   **240 fain** gladly   **243–244 still as** whenever
245–246 nightcaps (Scornful allusion to the *pilleus*, a felt cap worn by
the plebeians on festival days.)   **251 soft** i.e., wait a minute   **254 like**
likely.   **falling sickness** epilepsy. (But Cassius takes it to mean "falling
into servitude.")

CASSIUS
No, Caesar hath it not, but you and I,
And honest Casca, we have the falling sickness.

CASCA   I know not what you mean by that, but I am
sure Caesar fell down. If the tag-rag people did not   258
clap him and hiss him, according as he pleased and
displeased them, as they use to do the players in the   260
theater, I am no true man.   261

BRUTUS
What said he when he came unto himself?

CASCA   Marry, before he fell down, when he perceived
the common herd was glad he refused the crown, he
plucked me ope his doublet and offered them his throat   265
to cut. An I had been a man of any occupation, if I   266
would not have taken him at a word, I would I might
go to hell among the rogues. And so he fell. When he
came to himself again, he said if he had done or said
anything amiss, he desired their worships to think it
was his infirmity. Three or four wenches where I
stood cried, "Alas, good soul!" and forgave him with
all their hearts. But there's no heed to be taken of
them; if Caesar had stabbed their mothers they would   274
have done no less.

BRUTUS
And after that, he came thus sad away?   276

CASCA   Ay.

CASSIUS   Did Cicero say anything?

CASCA   Ay, he spoke Greek.

CASSIUS   To what effect?

CASCA   Nay, an I tell you that, I'll ne'er look you i' the
face again. But those that understood him smiled at
one another and shook their heads; but, for mine own
part, it was Greek to me. I could tell you more news
too. Marullus and Flavius, for pulling scarves off Cae-   285
sar's images, are put to silence. Fare you well. There   286
was more foolery yet, if I could remember it.

---

258 tag-rag ragtag, riffraff   **260 use** are accustomed   **261 true** honest   **265 plucked me ope** pulled open.   **doublet** Elizabethan upper
garment, like a jacket   **266 An** if.   **man . . . occupation** (1) working man
(2) man of action   **274 stabbed** (with bawdy connotation)   **276 sad**
seriously   **285 scarves** decorations, festoons   **286 put to silence** dismissed from office. (So reported in Plutarch.)

CASSIUS Will you sup with me tonight, Casca?

CASCA No, I am promised forth.   289

CASSIUS Will you dine with me tomorrow?

CASCA Ay, if I be alive, and your mind hold, and your
  dinner worth the eating.

CASSIUS Good. I will expect you.

CASCA Do so. Farewell both.   *Exit.*

BRUTUS
  What a blunt fellow is this grown to be!
  He was quick mettle when he went to school.   296

CASSIUS
  So is he now in execution
  Of any bold or noble enterprise,
  However he puts on this tardy form.   299
  This rudeness is a sauce to his good wit,   300
  Which gives men stomach to digest his words   301
  With better appetite.

BRUTUS
  And so it is. For this time I will leave you.
  Tomorrow, if you please to speak with me,
  I will come home to you; or, if you will,
  Come home to me, and I will wait for you.

CASSIUS
  I will do so. Till then, think of the world.   307
                                      Exit Brutus.
  Well, Brutus, thou art noble. Yet I see
  Thy honorable mettle may be wrought   309
  From that it is disposed. Therefore it is meet   310
  That noble minds keep ever with their likes;
  For who so firm that cannot be seduced?
  Caesar doth bear me hard, but he loves Brutus.   313

---

289 promised forth engaged to dine out   **296 quick mettle** of a lively
temperament   **299 However** however much.   **tardy form** appearance of
sluggishness   **300 rudeness** rough manner.   **wit** intellect   **301 stomach**
appetite, inclination   **307 the world** i.e., the state of the world
309 mettle (As often, the word combines the senses of *mettle*, temperament, and *metal*, substance. The latter meaning continues here in the
chemical metaphor of metal that is *wrought* or transmuted. As *honorable mettle* [or noble metal], gold cannot be transmuted into base
substances, and yet Cassius proposes to do just that with Brutus.
Compare 1.1.61.)   **309–310 wrought . . . disposed** i.e., turned away from
its natural disposition   **310 meet** fitting   **313 bear me hard** bear me a
grudge

If I were Brutus now, and he were Cassius,
He should not humor me. I will this night   315
In several hands in at his windows throw,   316
As if they came from several citizens,
Writings, all tending to the great opinion   318
That Rome holds of his name, wherein obscurely
Caesar's ambition shall be glancèd at.   320
And after this let Caesar seat him sure,   321
For we will shake him, or worse days endure.   *Exit.*

❖

1.3   *Thunder and lightning. Enter, [meeting,] Casca
[with his sword drawn] and Cicero.*

CICERO
  Good even, Casca. Brought you Caesar home?   1
  Why are you breathless? And why stare you so?
CASCA
  Are not you moved, when all the sway of earth   3
  Shakes like a thing unfirm? O Cicero,
  I have seen tempests when the scolding winds
  Have rived the knotty oaks, and I have seen   6
  Th' ambitious ocean swell and rage and foam
  To be exalted with the threatening clouds;   8
  But never till tonight, never till now,
  Did I go through a tempest dropping fire.
  Either there is a civil strife in heaven,
  Or else the world, too saucy with the gods,   12
  Incenses them to send destruction.
CICERO
  Why, saw you anything more wonderful?   14

315 **He** i.e., Brutus.   **humor** cajole (Cassius may be saying, if he, Brutus, were in my shoes, he wouldn't be so smug in his behavior toward
me as he is now; or, he wouldn't sway me as I sway him. Or he may
mean, if I were in Brutus' shoes, Caesar wouldn't cajole me so.)
316 **several hands** different handwriting   318 **tending to** concerning;
confirming   320 **glancèd** hinted   321 **seat him sure** seat himself se-
curely in power (i.e., watch out)

1.3. **Location: A street.**
1 **Brought** escorted   3 **sway** established order   6 **rived** split   8 **exalted
with** raised to the level of   12 **saucy** insolent   14 **more** else.   **wonderful** wondrous

CASCA
A common slave—you know him well by sight—
Held up his left hand, which did flame and burn
Like twenty torches joined, and yet his hand,
Not sensible of fire, remained unscorched.   18
Besides—I ha' not since put up my sword—   19
Against the Capitol I met a lion,   20
Who glazed upon me and went surly by   21
Without annoying me. And there were drawn   22
Upon a heap a hundred ghastly women,   23
Transformèd with their fear, who swore they saw
Men all in fire walk up and down the streets.
And yesterday the bird of night did sit   26
Even at noonday upon the marketplace,
Hooting and shrieking. When these prodigies   28
Do so conjointly meet, let not men say,   29
"These are their reasons, they are natural,"
For I believe they are portentous things
Unto the climate that they point upon.   32
CICERO
Indeed, it is a strange-disposèd time.
But men may construe things after their fashion,   34
Clean from the purpose of the things themselves.   35
Comes Caesar to the Capitol tomorrow?
CASCA
He doth; for he did bid An nius
Send word to you he wou l be there tomorrow.
CICERO
Good night then, Casca. his disturbèd sky
Is not to walk in.
CASCA   Farewell, Cicero.   *Exit Cicero.*

        Enter Cassius.

CASSIUS
Who's there?

18 **Not sensible of** not feeling   19 **put up** sheathed   20 **Against** opposite
or near   21 **glazed** stared glassily   22 **annoying** harming   22–23 **drawn
. . . heap** huddled together   23 **ghastly** pallid   26 **bird of night** owl, a
bird of evil omen   28 **prodigies** abnormalities, wonders   29 **conjointly
meet** coïncide   32 **climate** region   34 **construe** interpret.   **after their
fashion** in their own way   35 **Clean . . . purpose** contrary to the actual
import or meaning

CASCA   A Roman.
CASSIUS   Casca, by your voice.
CASCA
  Your ear is good. Cassius, what night is this!   42
CASSIUS
  A very pleasing night to honest men.
CASCA
  Who ever knew the heavens menace so?
CASSIUS
  Those that have known the earth so full of faults.
  For my part, I have walked about the streets,
  Submitting me unto the perilous night,
  And thus unbracèd, Casca, as you see,   48
  Have bared my bosom to the thunder-stone;   49
  And when the cross blue lightning seemed to open   50
  The breast of heaven, I did present myself
  Even in the aim and very flash of it.   52
CASCA
  But wherefore did you so much tempt the heavens?
  It is the part of men to fear and tremble   54
  When the most mighty gods by tokens send   55
  Such dreadful heralds to astonish us.   56
CASSIUS
  You are dull, Casca, and those sparks of life
  That should be in a Roman you do want,   58
  Or else you use not. You look pale, and gaze,
  And put on fear, and cast yourself in wonder,   60
  To see the strange impatience of the heavens.
  But if you would consider the true cause
  Why all these fires, why all these gliding ghosts,
  Why birds and beasts from quality and kind,   64
  Why old men, fools, and children calculate,   65
  Why all these things change from their ordinance,   66
  Their natures, and preformèd faculties,   67
  To monstrous quality—why, you shall find   68

42 what night what a night   **48 unbracèd** with doublet unfastened
49 thunder-stone thunderbolt   **50 cross** forked, jagged   **52 Even in the
aim** at the exact place at which it was aimed   **54 part** appropriate role
55 tokens signs   **56 astonish** stun   **58 want** lack   **60 put on** adopt, show
signs of   **64 from . . . kind** (behaving) contrary to their true nature
65 old men dotards.   **calculate** prophesy   **66 ordinance** established nature   **67 preformèd** innate, congenital   **68 monstrous** unnatural

That heaven hath infused them with these spirits
To make them instruments of fear and warning
Unto some monstrous state.   71
Now could I, Casca, name to thee a man
Most like this dreadful night,
That thunders, lightens, opens graves, and roars
As doth the lion in the Capitol—
A man no mightier than thyself or me
In personal action, yet prodigious grown   77
And fearful, as these strange eruptions are.   78

CASCA
'Tis Caesar that you mean, is it not, Cassius?

CASSIUS
Let it be who it is. For Romans now
Have thews and limbs like to their ancestors;   81
But, woe the while, our fathers' minds are dead,   82
And we are governed with our mothers' spirits.
Our yoke and sufferance show us womanish.   84

CASCA
Indeed, they say the senators tomorrow
Mean to establish Caesar as a king,
And he shall wear his crown by sea and land
In every place save here in Italy.

CASSIUS
I know where I will wear this dagger then;
Cassius from bondage will deliver Cassius.
Therein, ye gods, you make the weak most strong;   91
Therein, ye gods, you tyrants do defeat.
Nor stony tower, nor walls of beaten brass,   93
Nor airless dungeon, nor strong links of iron,
Can be retentive to the strength of spirit;   95
But life, being weary of these worldly bars,   96
Never lacks power to dismiss itself.
If I know this, know all the world besides,   98

---

71 monstrous state government or commonwealth in an unnatural
condition   **77 prodigious** ominous   **78 fearful** inspiring fear   **81 thews**
sinews, muscles.   **like** similar   **82 woe the while** alas for the age
84 yoke and sufferance patience under the yoke   **91 Therein** i.e., in the
ability to commit suicide   **93 Nor** neither   **95 be . . . spirit** confine a
resolute spirit   **96 bars** (1) prison bars (2) burdens (such as tyranny)
98 know . . . besides let the rest of the world know

That part of tyranny that I do bear
I can shake off at pleasure.   *Thunder still.*
CASCA   So can I.
  So every bondman in his own hand bears
  The power to cancel his captivity.
CASSIUS
  And why should Caesar be a tyrant, then?
  Poor man, I know he would not be a wolf
  But that he sees the Romans are but sheep;
  He were no lion, were not Romans hinds.   106
  Those that with haste will make a mighty fire
  Begin it with weak straws. What trash is Rome,
  What rubbish and what offal, when it serves   109
  For the base matter to illuminate   110
  So vile a thing as Caesar! But, O grief,
  Where hast thou led me? I perhaps speak this
  Before a willing bondman; then I know
  My answer must be made. But I am armed,   114
  And dangers are to me indifferent.   115
CASCA
  You speak to Casca, and to such a man
  That is no fleering telltale. Hold. My hand.   117
  Be factious for redress of all these griefs,   118
  And I will set this foot of mine as far
  As who goes farthest.   [*They shake hands.*]
CASSIUS   There's a bargain made.
  Now know you, Casca, I have moved already   121
  Some certain of the noblest-minded Romans
  To undergo with me an enterprise
  Of honorable-dangerous consequence;
  And I do know by this they stay for me   125
  In Pompey's porch. For now, this fearful night,   126

106 hinds (1) female of the red deer (2) servants, menials   **109 offal**
rubbish, wood shavings   **110 matter** i.e., fuel   **114 My answer . . . made**
I will have to answer (to Caesar) for what I have said.   **armed** (1) provided with weapons (2) morally fortified   **115 indifferent** unimportant
117 fleering sneering, scornful.   **Hold. My hand** enough; here is my
hand   **118 factious** active as a partisan.   **griefs** grievances   **121 moved**
urged   **125 by this** by this time.   **stay** wait   **126 Pompey's porch** the
colonnade of Pompey's great open theater, dedicated in 55 B.C. (Caesar
was assassinated there, though Shakespeare has the assassination take
place in the Capitol [i.e., the Senate chamber].)

There is no stir or walking in the streets,
And the complexion of the element   128
In favor's like the work we have in hand,   129
Most bloody, fiery, and most terrible.

    Enter Cinna.

CASCA
Stand close awhile, for here comes one in haste.   131
CASSIUS
'Tis Cinna; I do know him by his gait.
He is a friend.—Cinna, where haste you so?
CINNA
To find out you. Who's that? Metellus Cimber?
CASSIUS
No, it is Casca, one incorporate   135
To our attempts. Am I not stayed for, Cinna?
CINNA
I am glad on 't. What a fearful night is this!   137
There's two or three of us have seen strange sights.
CASSIUS   Am I not stayed for? Tell me.
CINNA
Yes, you are. O Cassius, if you could
But win the noble Brutus to our party—
CASSIUS
Be you content. Good Cinna, take this paper,
                         [Giving papers]
And look you lay it in the praetor's chair,   143
Where Brutus may but find it. And throw this   144
In at his window. Set this up with wax
Upon old Brutus' statue. All this done,   146
Repair to Pompey's porch, where you shall find us.   147
Is Decius Brutus and Trebonius there?
CINNA
All but Metellus Cimber, and he's gone
To seek you at your house. Well, I will hie,   150
And so bestow these papers as you bade me.

128 element sky   **129 favor's** appearance is   **131 close** concealed,
still   **135 incorporate** admitted as a member   **137 on 't** of it
 43 praetor's chair official seat of a praetor, Roman magistrate ranking
r ext below the consul. (Brutus was praetor, one of sixteen.)   **144 Where
. . it** where Brutus cannot help finding it   **146 old Brutus** (Lucius
Junius Brutus; Brutus was reputed to be his descendant.)   **147 Repair**
proceed (also in l. 152)   **150 hie** go quickly

CASSIUS
  That done, repair to Pompey's theater.   *Exit Cinna.*
  Come, Casca, you and I will yet ere day
  See Brutus at his house. Three parts of him   154
  Is ours already, and the man entire
  Upon the next encounter yields him ours.

CASCA
  O, he sits high in all the people's hearts;
  And that which would appear offense in us,
  His countenance, like richest alchemy,   159
  Will change to virtue and to worthiness.   160

CASSIUS
  Him and his worth, and our great need of him,
  You have right well conceited. Let us go,   162
  For it is after midnight, and ere day
  We will awake him and be sure of him.   *Exeunt.*

❧

154 parts i.e., quarters   **159 countenance** (1) support, approval (2) (honorable) appearance. **alchemy** pseudoscience the chief object of which was the transmutation of metals into gold   **160 virtue** (In addition to its literal meaning, a technical term for what the alchemists hoped to attain.)
162 conceited (1) conceived, grasped (2) expressed in a figure

2.1 *Enter Brutus in his orchard.*

BRUTUS What, Lucius, ho!—
I cannot by the progress of the stars
Give guess how near to day.—Lucius, I say!—
I would it were my fault to sleep so soundly.—
When, Lucius, when? Awake, I say! What, Lucius!

Enter Lucius.

LUCIUS Called you, my lord?
BRUTUS
Get me a taper in my study, Lucius.   7
When it is lighted, come and call me here.
LUCIUS I will, my lord.   *Exit.*
BRUTUS
It must be by his death. And for my part
I know no personal cause to spurn at him,   11
But for the general. He would be crowned.   12
How that might change his nature, there's the question.
It is the bright day that brings forth the adder,
And that craves wary walking. Crown him that,   15
And then I grant we put a sting in him
That at his will he may do danger with.
Th' abuse of greatness is when it disjoins
Remorse from power. And to speak truth of Caesar,   19
I have not known when his affections swayed   20
More than his reason. But 'tis a common proof   21
That lowliness is young ambition's ladder,   22
Whereto the climber-upward turns his face;
But when he once attains the upmost round   24
He then unto the ladder turns his back,
Looks in the clouds, scorning the base degrees   26
By which he did ascend. So Caesar may.
Then, lest he may, prevent. And since the quarrel

2.1. **Location:** Rome. Brutus' orchard, or garden.
7 **Get me** put.   **taper** candle   11 **spurn** kick   12 **general** general cause,
i.e., common good   15 **craves** requires.   **that** i.e., king, emperor
19 **Remorse** mercy, compassion   20 **affections** passions.   **swáyed**
ruled   21 **proof** experience   22 **lowliness** i.e., pretended humbleness
24 **round** rung   26 **base degrees** (1) lower rungs (2) persons of lower
social station

Will bear no color for the thing he is,   29
Fashion it thus: that what he is, augmented,   30
Would run to these and these extremities.
And therefore think him as a serpent's egg
Which, hatched, would, as his kind, grow mischievous; 33
And kill him in the shell.

    Enter Lucius.

LUCIUS
The taper burneth in your closet, sir.   35
Searching the window for a flint, I found
This paper, thus sealed up, and I am sure
It did not lie there when I went to bed.
                    Gives him the letter.

BRUTUS
Get you to bed again. It is not day.
Is not tomorrow, boy, the ides of March?   40
LUCIUS   I know not, sir.

BRUTUS
Look in the calendar and bring me word.
LUCIUS   I will, sir   *Exit.*

BRUTUS
The exhalations whizzing in the air   44
Give so much light that I may read by them.
             Opens the letter and reads.
"Brutus, thou sleep'st. Awake, and see thyself!
Shall Rome, et cetera? Speak, strike, redress!"
"Brutus, thou sleep'st. Awake!"
Such instigations have been often dropped
Where I have took them up.
"Shall Rome, et cetera?" Thus must I piece it out:
Shall Rome stand under one man's awe? What, Rome?
My ancestors did from the streets of Rome
The Tarquin drive, when he was called a king.
"Speak, strike, redress!" Am I entreated
To speak and strike? O Rome, I make thee promise, 56

29 Will . . . is i.e., can carry no appearance of justice so far as his
conduct to date is concerned **30 Fashion it** put the matter **33 as his
kind** according to his nature. **mischievous** harmful **35 closet** private
chamber, study **40 ides** fifteenth day **44 exhalations** meteors **56 I
make thee promise** I promise thee

If the redress will follow, thou receivest   57
Thy full petition at the hand of Brutus.

    Enter Lucius.

LUCIUS   Sir, March is wasted fifteen days. *Knock within.*
BRUTUS
  'Tis good. Go to the gate; somebody knocks.
                          [Exit Lucius.]
  Since Cassius first did whet me against Caesar,   61
  I have not slept.
  Between the acting of a dreadful thing
  And the first motion, all the interim is   64
  Like a phantasma or a hideous dream.   65
  The genius and the mortal instruments   66
  Are then in council; and the state of man,   67
  Like to a little kingdom, suffers then
  The nature of an insurrection.

    Enter Lucius.

LUCIUS
  Sir, 'tis your brother Cassius at the door,   70
  Who doth desire to see you.
BRUTUS   Is he alone?
LUCIUS
  No, sir, there are more with him.
BRUTUS   Do you know them?
LUCIUS
  No, sir. Their hats are plucked about their ears,
  And half their faces buried in their cloaks,
  That by no means I may discover them   75
  By any mark of favor.
BRUTUS   Let 'em enter.   *[Exit Lucius.]* 76
  They are the faction. O conspiracy,
  Sham'st thou to show thy dangerous brow by night,

---

57 If . . . follow i.e., if striking Caesar will lead to the reform of grievances **61 whet** incite **64 motion** proposal **65 phantasma** hallucina-
tion **66–67 The genius . . . council** i.e., the immortal part of man, his
rational soul, deliberates or debates with his lower or mortal faculties,
his physical and passionate side **67 state of man** i.e., man as a microcosm, a tiny kingdom **70 brother** i.e., brother-in-law. (Cassius had
married a sister of Brutus.) **75 discover** identify **76 favor** appearance

When evils are most free? O, then by day   79
Where wilt thou find a cavern dark enough
To mask thy monstrous visage? Seek none, conspiracy!
Hide it in smiles and affability;
For if thou path, thy native semblance on,   83
Not Erebus itself were dim enough   84
To hide thee from prevention.   85

>   *Enter the conspirators, Cassius, Casca, Decius,*
>   *Cinna, Metellus [Cimber], and Trebonius.*

CASSIUS
I think we are too bold upon your rest.   86
Good morrow, Brutus. Do we trouble you?
BRUTUS
I have been up this hour, awake all night.
Know I these men that come along with you?
CASSIUS
Yes, every man of them, and no man here
But honors you; and every one doth wish
You had but that opinion of yourself
Which every noble Roman bears of you.
This is Trebonius.
BRUTUS   He is welcome hither.
CASSIUS
This, Decius Brutus.
BRUTUS   He is welcome too.
CASSIUS
This, Casca; this, Cinna; and this, Metellus Cimber.
BRUTUS   They are all welcome.
What watchful cares do interpose themselves   98
Betwixt your eyes and night?
CASSIUS   Shall I entreat a word?
>   *They [Brutus and Cassius] whisper.*
DECIUS
Here lies the east. Doth not the day break here?
CASCA   No.

---

79 free free to roam at will   **83 path** proceed, walk about.   **thy . . . on**
wearing your true appearance   **84 Erebus** region of darkness between
earth and Hades   **85 prevention** detection and being forestalled
86 upon in intruding upon   **98 watchful cares** worries preventing sleep

CINNA
   O, pardon, sir, it doth; and yon gray lines
   That fret the clouds are messengers of day.   104
CASCA
   You shall confess that you are both deceived.   105
   Here, as I point my sword, the sun arises,
   Which is a great way growing on the south,   107
   Weighing the youthful season of the year.   108
   Some two months hence, up higher toward the north
   He first presents his fire; and the high east   110
   Stands, as the Capitol, directly here.
BRUTUS [*Coming forward*]
   Give me your hands all over, one by one.   112
CASSIUS
   And let us swear our resolution.
BRUTUS
   No, not an oath. If not the face of men,   114
   The sufferance of our souls, the time's abuse—   115
   If these be motives weak, break off betimes,   116
   And every man hence to his idle bed;   117
   So let high-sighted tyranny range on   118
   Till each man drop by lottery. But if these,   119
   As I am sure they do, bear fire enough
   To kindle cowards and to steel with valor
   The melting spirits of women, then, countrymen,
   What need we any spur but our own cause
   To prick us to redress? What other bond   124
   Than secret Romans that have spoke the word
   And will not palter? And what other oath   126
   Than honesty to honesty engaged   127
   That this shall be or we will fall for it?
   Swear priests and cowards and men cautelous,   129

104 fret mark with interlacing lines   **105 deceived** mistaken
107 growing on toward   **108 Weighing** considering, in consequence of
110 high due   **112 all over** one and all   **114 face of men** i.e., grave look of
all concerned persons in the state   **115 sufferance** state of suffering.
time's abuse corruptions of the present day   **116 betimes** at once
117 idle unused, empty   **118 high-sighted** upward-gazing (cf. 2.1.26); or
haughty, looking down from an Olympian height   **119 by lottery** i.e., as
the capricious tyrant chances to pick on him.   **these** i.e., these injustices
just cited   **124 prick** spur   **126 palter** use trickery   **127 honesty** personal
honor   **129 Swear** make swear.   **cautelous** deceitful; cautious

Old feeble carrions, and such suffering souls   130
That welcome wrongs; unto bad causes swear
Such creatures as men doubt; but do not stain
The even virtue of our enterprise,   133
Nor th' insuppressive mettle of our spirits,   134
To think that or our cause or our performance   135
Did need an oath, when every drop of blood
That every Roman bears—and nobly bears—
Is guilty of a several bastardy   138
If he do break the smallest particle
Of any promise that hath passed from him.

CASSIUS
But what of Cicero? Shall we sound him?   141
I think he will stand very strong with us.

CASCA
Let us not leave him out.

CINNA   No, by no means.

METELLUS
O, let us have him, for his silver hairs
Will purchase us a good opinion   145
And buy men's voices to commend our deeds.
It shall be said his judgment ruled our hands;
Our youths and wildness shall no whit appear,
But all be buried in his gravity.

BRUTUS
O, name him not. Let us not break with him,   150
For he will never follow anything
That other men begin.

CASSIUS   Then leave him out.

CASCA   Indeed he is not fit.

DECIUS
Shall no man else be touched but only Caesar?

CASSIUS
Decius, well urged. I think it is not meet   156

130 **carrions** men who resemble corpses.   **suffering** long-suffering
133 **even** steadfast, consistent   134 **insuppressive** not to be sup-
pressed   135 **or . . . or** either . . . or   138 **several bastardy** i.e., individual dishonorable act. (A noble Roman failing to keep his promise
would be charged with a separate desecration of his birthright for
each drop of blood in his body.)   141 **sound him** find out his feelings   145 **purchase** procure (playing on *silver* in l. 144 as money)
150 **break with** confide in   156 **meet** fitting

Mark Antony, so well beloved of Caesar,
Should outlive Caesar. We shall find of him   158
A shrewd contriver; and you know his means,
If he improve them, may well stretch so far   160
As to annoy us all. Which to prevent,   161
Let Antony and Caesar fall together.

BRUTUS
Our course will seem too bloody, Caius Cassius,
To cut the head off and then hack the limbs,
Like wrath in death and envy afterwards;   165
For Antony is but a limb of Caesar.
Let's be sacrificers, but not butchers, Caius.
We all stand up against the spirit of Caesar,
And in the spirit of men there is no blood.
O, that we then could come by Caesar's spirit   170
And not dismember Caesar! But, alas,
Caesar must bleed for it. And, gentle friends,   172
Let's kill him boldly but not wrathfully;
Let's carve him as a dish fit for the gods,
Not hew him as a carcass fit for hounds.
And let our hearts, as subtle masters do,
Stir up their servants to an act of rage   177
And after seem to chide 'em. This shall make
Our purpose necessary, and not envious;   179
Which so appearing to the common eyes,
We shall be called purgers, not murderers.
And for Mark Antony, think not of him;
For he can do no more than Caesar's arm
When Caesar's head is off.

CASSIUS   Yet I fear him,
For in the engrafted love he bears to Caesar—   185

BRUTUS
Alas, good Cassius, do not think of him.
If he love Caesar, all that he can do
Is to himself—take thought and die for Caesar.   188
And that were much he should, for he is given   189
To sports, to wildness, and much company.

158 of in   **160 improve** exploit, make good use of   **161 annoy** injure
165 envy malice   **170 come by** get hold of   **172 gentle** noble   **177 their
servants** i.e., our hands   **179 envious** malicious   **185 engrafted** firmly
implanted   **188 take thought** become melancholy   **189 much he should**
more than is to be expected of him, hence unlikely

TREBONIUS
　There is no fear in him. Let him not die,   191
　For he will live, and laugh at this hereafter.   192
                              Clock strikes.

BRUTUS
　Peace! Count the clock.
CASSIUS   The clock hath stricken three.
TREBONIUS
　'Tis time to part.
CASSIUS   But it is doubtful yet
　Whether Caesar will come forth today or no;
　For he is superstitious grown of late,
　Quite from the main opinion he held once   197
　Of fantasy, of dreams, and ceremonies.
　It may be these apparent prodigies,   199
　The unaccustomed terror of this night,
　And the persuasion of his augurers
　May hold him from the Capitol today.

DECIUS
　Never fear that. If he be so resolved,
　I can o'ersway him; for he loves to hear
　That unicorns may be betrayed with trees,   205
　And bears with glasses, elephants with holes,   206
　Lions with toils, and men with flatterers;   207
　But when I tell him he hates flatterers,
　He says he does, being then most flattered.
　Let me work;
　For I can give his humor the true bent,   211
　And I will bring him to the Capitol.

CASSIUS
　Nay, we will all of us be there to fetch him.
BRUTUS
　By the eighth hour. Is that the uttermost?   214
CINNA
　Be that the uttermost, and fail not then.

191 no fear nothing to fear　**192 s.d. Clock strikes** (A much-commented-upon anachronism; the mechanical clock was not invented until c.1300.)
197 from the main contrary to the strong　**199 apparent** obvious
205 unicorns . . . trees i.e., by having the unicorn imprison itself by driving its horn into a tree as it charges at the hunter　**206 glasses** mirrors (enabling the hunter to approach the bear while it vainly admires itself in the mirror).　**holes** pitfalls　**207 toils** nets, snares　**211 humor** disposition.　**true bent** right direction　**214 uttermost** latest

METELLUS
  Caius Ligarius doth bear Caesar hard,   216
  Who rated him for speaking well of Pompey.   217
  I wonder none of you have thought of him.
BRUTUS
  Now, good Metellus, go along by him.   219
  He loves me well, and I have given him reasons;   220
  Send him but hither, and I'll fashion him.   221
CASSIUS
  The morning comes upon 's. We'll leave you, Brutus.
  And, friends, disperse yourselves; but all remember
  What you have said, and show yourselves true Romans.
BRUTUS
  Good gentlemen, look fresh and merrily;
  Let not our looks put on our purposes,   226
  But bear it as our Roman actors do,
  With untired spirits and formal constancy.   228
  And so good morrow to you every one.   229

                    Exeunt. Manet Brutus.

  Boy! Lucius! Fast asleep? It is no matter.   230
  Enjoy the honey-heavy dew of slumber.
  Thou hast no figures nor no fantasies   232
  Which busy care draws in the brains of men;
  Therefore thou sleep'st so sound.

    Enter Portia.

PORTIA   Brutus, my lord!
BRUTUS
  Portia, what mean you? Wherefore rise you now?
  It is not for your health thus to commit
  Your weak condition to the raw cold morning.
PORTIA
  Nor for yours neither. You've ungently, Brutus,   238
  Stole from my bed. And yesternight, at supper,
  You suddenly arose, and walked about

216 bear Caesar hard bear a grudge toward Caesar   **217 rated** angrily rebuked   **219 by him** by way of his house   **220 reasons** i.e., for loving me   **221 fashion** shape (to our purposes)   **226 put on** display, wear in open view   **228 formal constancy** steadfast appearance, decorum **229 s.d. Manet** he remains onstage   **230 Lucius** (Brutus calls to his servant, who is evidently within, asleep, after having admitted the conspirators at l. 85; later, at l. 310, he is still within when Brutus calls to him.) **232 figures** imaginings   **238 ungently** discourteously, unkindly

Musing and sighing, with your arms across,   241
And when I asked you what the matter was,
You stared upon me with ungentle looks.
I urged you further; then you scratched your head
And too impatiently stamped with your foot.
Yet I insisted, yet you answered not,   246
But with an angry wafture of your hand   247
Gave sign for me to leave you. So I did,
Fearing to strengthen that impatience
Which seemed too much enkindled, and withal   250
Hoping it was but an effect of humor,   251
Which sometimes hath his hour with every man.   252
It will not let you eat, nor talk, nor sleep,
And could it work so much upon your shape
As it hath much prevailed on your condition,   255
I should not know you Brutus. Dear my lord,   256
Make me acquainted with your cause of grief.

BRUTUS

I am not well in health, and that is all.

PORTIA

Brutus is wise and, were he not in health,
He would embrace the means to come by it.

BRUTUS

Why, so I do. Good Portia, go to bed.   261

PORTIA

Is Brutus sick? And is it physical   262
To walk unbracèd and suck up the humors   263
Of the dank morning? What, is Brutus sick,
And will he steal out of his wholesome bed
To dare the vile contagion of the night,
And tempt the rheumy and unpurgèd air   267
To add unto his sickness? No, my Brutus,
You have some sick offense within your mind,   269
Which by the right and virtue of my place

241 across folded (A sign of melancholy.) **246 Yet . . . yet** still . . .
still **247 wafture** waving **250 withal** indeed **251 humor** mood
252 his its **255 condition** inner state of mind **256 know you** recognize you as **261 so I do** (Said with a double meaning not perceived by
Portia: I seek through Caesar's death the means to better the health of
the state.) **262 physical** healthful **263 unbracèd** with loosened
clothing. **humors** damps, mists **267 rheumy** damp. **unpurgèd**
not purified (by the sun) **269 sick offense** harmful disturbance

I ought to know of. [*She kneels.*] And upon my knees
I charm you, by my once-commended beauty,   272
By all your vows of love, and that great vow
Which did incorporate and make us one,
That you unfold to me, your self, your half,
Why you are heavy, and what men tonight   276
Have had resort to you; for here have been   277
Some six or seven, who did hide their faces
Even from darkness.

BRUTUS   Kneel not, gentle Portia.
                              [*He raises her.*]

PORTIA
I should not need if you were gentle Brutus.
Within the bond of marriage, tell me, Brutus,
Is it excepted I should know no secrets   282
That appertain to you? Am I your self
But as it were in sort or limitation,   284
To keep with you at meals, comfort your bed,   285
And talk to you sometimes? Dwell I but in the suburbs   286
Of your good pleasure? If it be no more,
Portia is Brutus' harlot, not his wife.

BRUTUS
You are my true and honorable wife,
As dear to me as are the ruddy drops
That visit my sad heart.

PORTIA
If this were true, then should I know this secret.
I grant I am a woman, but withal   293
A woman that Lord Brutus took to wife.
I grant I am a woman, but withal
A woman well-reputed, Cato's daughter.   296
Think you I am no stronger than my sex,
Being so fathered and so husbanded?
Tell me your counsels, I will not disclose 'em.   299

---

272 **charm** conjure, entreat   276 **heavy** sad   277 **had resort to** visited
282 **excepted** made an exception that   284 **in . . . limitation** only up to a
point   285 **keep** stay, be   286 **suburbs** periphery. (In Elizabethan
London, prostitutes frequented the suburbs.)   293 **withal** in addition
296 **Cato's daughter** (Cato of Utica was famous for his integrity; he
sided with Pompey against Caesar in 48 B.C. and later killed himself
rather than submit to Caesar's tyranny. He was Brutus' uncle as well as
his father-in-law.)   299 **counsels** secrets

I have made strong proof of my constancy,
Giving myself a voluntary wound
Here, in the thigh. Can I bear that with patience,
And not my husband's secrets?

BRUTUS   O ye gods,
Render me worthy of this noble wife!

                                    Knock [within].
Hark, hark, one knocks. Portia, go in awhile,
And by and by thy bosom shall partake
The secrets of my heart.
All my engagements I will construe to thee,   308
All the charactery of my sad brows.   309
Leave me with haste.   *Exit Portia.*
          Lucius, who's that knocks?

*Enter Lucius and [Caius] Ligarius [wearing a
kerchief].*

LUCIUS
Here is a sick man that would speak with you.   311
BRUTUS
Caius Ligarius, that Metellus spake of.
Boy, stand aside. [*Exit Lucius.*] Caius Ligarius, how?   313
LIGARIUS
Vouchsafe good morrow from a feeble tongue.   314
BRUTUS
O, what a time have you chose out, brave Caius,   315
To wear a kerchief! Would you were not sick!
LIGARIUS
I am not sick, if Brutus have in hand
Any exploit worthy the name of honor.
BRUTUS
Such an exploit have I in hand, Ligarius,
Had you a healthful ear to hear of it.
LIGARIUS
By all the gods that Romans bow before,
I here discard my sickness! Soul of Rome!
                    [*He throws off his kerchief.*]

308 construe explain fully   **309 charactery** handwriting, i.e., what is
figured there   **311 sick man** (In Elizabethan medicine, not Roman, a
poultice was often applied to the forehead of a patient and wrapped in a
handkerchief; hence the kerchief in l. 316.)   **313 how** i.e., how are you
314 Vouchsafe deign (to accept)   **315 brave** noble

Brave son, derived from honorable loins!
Thou like an exorcist hast conjured up   324
My mortifièd spirit. Now bid me run,   325
And I will strive with things impossible,
Yea, get the better of them. What's to do?

BRUTUS
A piece of work that will make sick men whole.   328

LIGARIUS
But are not some whole that we must make sick?

BRUTUS
That must we also. What it is, my Caius,
I shall unfold to thee as we are going
To whom it must be done.

LIGARIUS   Set on your foot,   332
And with a heart new-fired I follow you
To do I know not what; but it sufficeth
That Brutus leads me on.   *Thunder.*

BRUTUS   Follow me, then.   *Exeunt.*

❖

2.2   *Thunder and lightning. Enter Julius Caesar, in
his nightgown.*

CAESAR
Nor heaven nor earth have been at peace tonight.   1
Thrice hath Calpurnia in her sleep cried out,
"Help, ho, they murder Caesar!"—Who's within?

Enter a Servant.

SERVANT   My lord?

CAESAR
Go bid the priests do present sacrifice   5
And bring me their opinions of success.   6

SERVANT   I will, my lord.   *Exit.*

---

324 exorcist conjurer   **325 mortifièd** deadened   **328 whole** healthy, i.e.,
free of the disease of tyranny   **332 To whom** i.e., to him to whom

2.2. Location: Caesar's house.
s.d. nightgown dressing gown   **1 Nor** neither   **5 present** immediate.
sacrifice examination of the entrails of sacrificed animals for omens
6 success the result, what will follow

Enter Calpurnia.

CALPURNIA
What mean you, Caesar? Think you to walk forth?
You shall not stir out of your house today.

CAESAR
Caesar shall forth. The things that threatened me   10
Ne'er looked but on my back. When they shall see
The face of Caesar, they are vanishèd.

CALPURNIA
Caesar, I never stood on ceremonies,   13
Yet now they fright me. There is one within,
Besides the things that we have heard and seen,
Recounts most horrid sights seen by the watch.   16
A lioness hath whelpèd in the streets,   17
And graves have yawned and yielded up their dead.   18
Fierce fiery warriors fight upon the clouds   19
In ranks and squadrons and right form of war,   20
Which drizzled blood upon the Capitol.
The noise of battle hurtled in the air;   22
Horses did neigh, and dying men did groan,
And ghosts did shriek and squeal about the streets.
O Caesar, these things are beyond all use,   25
And I do fear them.

CAESAR   What can be avoided
Whose end is purposed by the mighty gods?
Yet Caesar shall go forth; for these predictions
Are to the world in general as to Caesar.   29

CALPURNIA
When beggars die there are no comets seen;
The heavens themselves blaze forth the death of princes.   31

CAESAR
Cowards die many times before their deaths;
The valiant never taste of death but once.
Of all the wonders that I yet have heard,
It seems to me most strange that men should fear,

---

10 forth go forth   **13 stood on ceremonies** attached importance to
omens   **16 watch** (An anachronism, since there was no *watch*, or body
of night watchmen, in Caesar's Rome.)   **17 whelpèd** given birth
18 yawned gaped   **19 fight** did fight   **20 right form** regular formation
22 hurtled clashed   **25 use** normal experience   **29 Are to** are as appli-
cable to   **31 blaze forth** proclaim (in a blaze of light)

Seeing that death, a necessary end,
Will come when it will come.

    Enter a Servant.

                            What say the augurers?

SERVANT
They would not have you to stir forth today.
Plucking the entrails of an offering forth,
They could not find a heart within the beast.

CAESAR
The gods do this in shame of cowardice.
Caesar should be a beast without a heart
If he should stay at home today for fear.
No, Caesar shall not. Danger knows full well
That Caesar is more dangerous than he.
We are two lions littered in one day,
And I the elder and more terrible;
And Caesar shall go forth.

CALPURNIA   Alas, my lord,
Your wisdom is consumed in confidence.   49
Do not go forth today! Call it my fear
That keeps you in the house, and not your own.
We'll send Mark Antony to the Senate House,
And he shall say you are not well today.
Let me, upon my knee, prevail in this.   *[She kneels.]*

CAESAR
Mark Antony shall say I am not well,
And for thy humor I will stay at home.   56

                         [He raises her.]

    Enter Decius.

Here's Decius Brutus. He shall tell them so.

DECIUS
Caesar, all hail! Good morrow, worthy Caesar.
I come to fetch you to the Senate House.

CAESAR
And you are come in very happy time   60
To bear my greeting to the senators
And tell them that I will not come today.

49 consumed in confidence destroyed by overconfidence **56 humor**
whim **60 happy** opportune

Cannot, is false, and that I dare not, falser;
I will not come today. Tell them so, Decius.

CALPURNIA
Say he is sick.

CAESAR   Shall Caesar send a lie?
Have I in conquest stretched mine arm so far
To be afeard to tell graybeards the truth?
Decius, go tell them Caesar will not come.

DECIUS
Most mighty Caesar, let me know some cause,
Lest I be laughed at when I tell them so.

CAESAR
The cause is in my will: I will not come.
That is enough to satisfy the Senate.
But for your private satisfaction,
Because I love you, I will let you know.
Calpurnia here, my wife, stays me at home.   75
She dreamt tonight she saw my statue,   76
Which like a fountain with an hundred spouts
Did run pure blood; and many lusty Romans   78
Came smiling and did bathe their hands in it.
And these does she apply for warnings and portents   80
And evils imminent, and on her knee
Hath begged that I will stay at home today.

DECIUS
This dream is all amiss interpreted;
It was a vision fair and fortunate.
Your statue spouting blood in many pipes,
In which so many smiling Romans bathed,
Signifies that from you great Rome shall suck
Reviving blood, and that great men shall press   88
For tinctures, stains, relics, and cognizance.   89
This by Calpurnia's dream is signified.

CAESAR
And this way have you well expounded it.

75 **stays** detains 76 **tonight** last night 78 **lusty** lively, merry 80 **apply for** interpret as 88 **press** crowd around 89 **tinctures** handkerchiefs dipped in the blood of martyrs, with healing powers; or colors in a coat of arms. (*Tinctures, stains,* and *relics* are all venerated properties, as though Caesar were a saint.) **cognizance** heraldic emblems worn by a nobleman's followers

DECIUS
I have, when you have heard what I can say;
And know it now. The Senate have concluded
To give this day a crown to mighty Caesar.
If you shall send them word you will not come,
Their minds may change. Besides, it were a mock   96
Apt to be rendered for someone to say   97
"Break up the Senate till another time
When Caesar's wife shall meet with better dreams."
If Caesar hide himself, shall they not whisper
"Lo, Caesar is afraid"?
Pardon me, Caesar, for my dear dear love
To your proceeding bids me tell you this,   103
And reason to my love is liable.   104

CAESAR
How foolish do your fears seem now, Calpurnia!
I am ashamèd I did yield to them.
Give me my robe, for I will go.

    Enter Brutus, Ligarius, Metellus, Casca,
    Trebonius, Cinna, and Publius.

And look where Publius is come to fetch me.

PUBLIUS
Good morrow, Caesar.

CAESAR   Welcome, Publius.
What, Brutus, are you stirred so early too?
Good morrow, Casca. Caius Ligarius,
Caesar was ne'er so much your enemy
As that same ague which hath made you lean.   113
What is 't o'clock?

BRUTUS   Caesar, 'tis strucken eight.

CAESAR
I thank you for your pains and courtesy.

    Enter Antony.

See, Antony, that revels long o' nights,
Is notwithstanding up. Good morrow, Antony.

ANTONY So to most noble Caesar.

96–97 mock . . . rendered witty remark apt to be made **103 proceeding**
advancement **104 reason . . . liable** my reason or sense of propriety is
overruled by my love **113 ague** fever

CAESAR [*To a Servant*]   Bid them prepare within.   119
                                        [*Exit Servant.*]
    I am to blame to be thus waited for.
    Now, Cinna. Now, Metellus. What, Trebonius,
    I have an hour's talk in store for you;
    Remember that you call on me today.
    Be near me, that I may remember you.
TREBONIUS
    Caesar, I will. [*Aside.*] And so near will I be
    That your best friends shall wish I had been further.
CAESAR
    Good friends, go in and taste some wine with me,
    And we, like friends, will straightway go together.
BRUTUS [*Aside*]
    That every like is not the same, O Caesar,   129
    The heart of Brutus earns to think upon!   *Exeunt.* 130

❖

2.3   *Enter Artemidorus [reading a paper].*

ARTEMIDORUS   "Caesar, beware of Brutus; take heed of
    Cassius; come not near Casca; have an eye to Cinna;
    trust not Trebonius; mark well Metellus Cimber; De-
    cius Brutus loves thee not; thou hast wronged Caius
    Ligarius. There is but one mind in all these men, and
    it is bent against Caesar. If thou beest not immortal, 6
    look about you. Security gives way to conspiracy. The 7
    mighty gods defend thee! Thy lover,   8
                                        Artemidorus."
    Here will I stand till Caesar pass along,
    And as a suitor will I give him this.   11
    My heart laments that virtue cannot live

---

119 prepare within i.e., set out a repast of wine in the other room, or
prepare to leave. (Perhaps addressed to the servant who entered at
l. 37, or to Calpurnia.)   **129 That . . . same** i.e., that everyone who seems
a friend is not actually so. (Proverbial.)   **130 earns** grieves

2.3. Location: A street near the Capitol.
6 bent directed   **7 Security** overconfidence.   **gives way** opens a path
8 lover friend   **11 as a suitor** as if I were a petitioner

Out of the teeth of emulation.　　　　　　　　　　13
If thou read this, O Caesar, thou mayest live;
If not, the Fates with traitors do contrive.　　　*Exit.* 15

❖

2.4　　*Enter Portia and Lucius.*

PORTIA
　I prithee, boy, run to the Senate House.
　Stay not to answer me, but get thee gone.—
　Why dost thou stay?
LUCIUS　　　　　　　　To know my errand, madam.
PORTIA
　I would have had thee there and here again
　Ere I can tell thee what thou shouldst do there.
　[*Aside.*] O constancy, be strong upon my side;　　6
　Set a huge mountain 'tween my heart and tongue!
　I have a man's mind, but a woman's might.
　How hard it is for women to keep counsel!—　　9
　Art thou here yet?
LUCIUS　　　　　　Madam, what should I do?
　Run to the Capitol, and nothing else?
　And so return to you, and nothing else?
PORTIA
　Yes, bring me word, boy, if thy lord look well,
　For he went sickly forth; and take good note　　14
　What Caesar doth, what suitors press to him.
　Hark, boy, what noise is that?
LUCIUS　　I hear none, madam.
PORTIA　　Prithee, listen well.
　I heard a bustling rumor, like a fray,　　　　　19
　And the wind brings it from the Capitol.
LUCIUS　　Sooth, madam, I hear nothing.　　　　21

　　　　Enter the Soothsayer.

13 **Out . . . emulation** i.e., beyond the reach of grudging envy
15 **contrive** conspire

2.4. Location: Before the house of Brutus.
6 **constancy** resolution　9 **counsel** a secret　14 **take good note** observe
closely　19 **bustling rumor** confused sound　21 **Sooth** truly

PORTIA

Come hither, fellow. Which way hast thou been?

SOOTHSAYER   At mine own house, good lady.

PORTIA

What is 't o'clock?

SOOTHSAYER   About the ninth hour, lady.   24

PORTIA

Is Caesar yet gone to the Capitol?

SOOTHSAYER

Madam, not yet. I go to take my stand,
To see him pass on to the Capitol.

PORTIA

Thou hast some suit to Caesar, hast thou not?

SOOTHSAYER

That I have, lady, if it will please Caesar
To be so good to Caesar as to hear me:
I shall beseech him to befriend himself.

PORTIA

Why, know'st thou any harms intended towards him?

SOOTHSAYER

None that I know will be, much that I fear may chance.
Good morrow to you. Here the street is narrow.
The throng that follows Caesar at the heels,
Of senators, of praetors, common suitors,   36
Will crowd a feeble man almost to death.
I'll get me to a place more void, and there   38
Speak to great Caesar as he comes along.   *Exit.*

PORTIA

I must go in. Ay me, how weak a thing
The heart of woman is! O Brutus,
The heavens speed thee in thine enterprise!
Sure, the boy heard me.—Brutus hath a suit
That Caesar will not grant.—O, I grow faint.—
Run, Lucius, and commend me to my lord;
Say I am merry. Come to me again
And bring me word what he doth say to thee.
                              Exeunt [separately].

✣

24 **the ninth hour** i.e., 9 A.M. (In Roman reckoning the ninth hour would
be 3 P.M.)   36 **praetors** judges   38 **void** empty, uncrowded

3.1 *Flourish. Enter Caesar, Brutus, Cassius, Casca,*
Decius, Metellus [Cimber], Trebonius, Cinna,
Antony, Lepidus, Artemidorus, Publius,
[Popilius Lena,] and the Soothsayer; [others
following].

CAESAR [*To the Soothsayer*]   The ides of March are come.
SOOTHSAYER   Ay, Caesar, but not gone.
ARTEMIDORUS   Hail, Caesar! Read this schedule.   3
DECIUS
Trebonius doth desire you to o'erread,
At your best leisure, this his humble suit.
ARTEMIDORUS
O Caesar, read mine first, for mine's a suit
That touches Caesar nearer. Read it, great Caesar.
CAESAR
What touches us ourself shall be last served.
ARTEMIDORUS
Delay not, Caesar, read it instantly.
CAESAR
What, is the fellow mad?
PUBLIUS   Sirrah, give place.   10
CASSIUS
What, urge you your petitions in the street?
Come to the Capitol.

[*Caesar goes to the Capitol and takes his place,*
the rest following.]

POPILIUS [*To Cassius*]
I wish your enterprise today may thrive.
CASSIUS   What enterprise, Popilius?
POPILIUS [*To Cassius*]   Fare you well.
                              [*He advances to Caesar.*]
BRUTUS   What said Popilius Lena?
CASSIUS
He wished today our enterprise might thrive.
I fear our purpose is discoverèd.

3.1. Location: Before the Capitol, and, following l. 12, within the
Capitol.
s.d. others following (Citizens may be present, though not certainly so;
see ll. 83 and 93–94.)   **3 schedule** document   **10 Sirrah** fellow. (A form
of address to a social inferior.)   **place** way

BRUTUS
Look how he makes to Caesar. Mark him.   19
                    [*Popilius speaks apart to Caesar.*]

CASSIUS
Casca, be sudden, for we fear prevention.   20
Brutus, what shall be done? If this be known,
Cassius or Caesar never shall turn back,   22
For I will slay myself.

BRUTUS   Cassius, be constant.   23
Popilius Lena speaks not of our purposes;
For look, he smiles, and Caesar doth not change.   25

CASSIUS
Trebonius knows his time, for look you, Brutus,
He draws Mark Antony out of the way.
                    [*Exit Trebonius with Antony.*]

DECIUS
Where is Metellus Cimber? Let him go
And presently prefer his suit to Caesar.   29

BRUTUS
He is addressed. Press near and second him.   30

CINNA
Casca, you are the first that rears your hand.
                    [*They press near Caesar.*]

CAESAR
Are we all ready? What is now amiss
That Caesar and his Senate must redress?

METELLUS [*Kneeling*]
Most high, most mighty, and most puissant Caesar,
Metellus Cimber throws before thy seat
An humble heart—

CAESAR   I must prevent thee, Cimber.   36
These couchings and these lowly courtesies   37
Might fire the blood of ordinary men,   38
And turn preordinance and first decree   39
Into the law of children. Be not fond   40

19 **makes to** advances toward   20 **sudden** swift in action.   **prevention** being forestalled   22 **turn back** i.e., return alive   23 **constant** resolute   25 **change** change expression   29 **presently prefer** immediately present   30 **addressed** ready   36 **prevent** forestall   37 **couchings, lowly courtesies** submissive bows   38 **fire the blood of** incite   39 **preordinance . . . decree** matters already firmly decided   40 **law of children** i.e., laws to be changed as children change rules in their games.   **fond** so foolish as

To think that Caesar bears such rebel blood   41
That will be thawed from the true quality   42
With that which melteth fools—I mean, sweet words,
Low-crookèd curtsies, and base spaniel fawning.   44
Thy brother by decree is banishèd.
If thou dost bend and pray and fawn for him,   46
I spurn thee like a cur out of my way.   47
Know, Caesar doth not wrong, nor without cause
Will he be satisfied.

METELLUS
Is there no voice more worthy than my own
To sound more sweetly in great Caesar's ear
For the repealing of my banished brother?   52

BRUTUS [*Kneeling*]
I kiss thy hand, but not in flattery, Caesar,
Desiring thee that Publius Cimber may
Have an immediate freedom of repeal.   55

CAESAR
What, Brutus?

CASSIUS [*Kneeling*]   Pardon, Caesar! Caesar, pardon!
As low as to thy foot doth Cassius fall,
To beg enfranchisement for Publius Cimber.   58

CAESAR
I could be well moved, if I were as you;
If I could pray to move, prayers would move me.   60
But I am constant as the northern star,   61
Of whose true-fixed and resting quality   62
There is no fellow in the firmament.   63
The skies are painted with unnumbered sparks;
They are all fire and every one doth shine;
But there's but one in all doth hold his place.
So in the world: 'tis furnished well with men,
And men are flesh and blood, and apprehensive;   68
Yet in the number I do know but one

41 rebel i.e., rebellious against the law and against his own firm nature   **42 true quality** i.e., proper firmness and stability   **44 Low-
crookèd** bent low   **46 bend** bow   **47 spurn** kick   **52 repealing** recall
55 freedom of repeal permission to be recalled   **58 enfranchisement**
liberation (from the decree of banishment)   **60 pray to move** make
petition (as you do)   **61 northern star** polestar   **62 true-fixed** firmly
fixed, unmovable.   **resting** unchanging   **63 fellow** equal
68 apprehensive capable of perception

That unassailable holds on his rank,   70
Unshaked of motion. And that I am he,   71
Let me a little show it even in this—
That I was constant Cimber should be banished,
And constant do remain to keep him so.

CINNA [*Kneeling*]
   O Caesar—

CAESAR   Hence! Wilt thou lift up Olympus?   75

DECIUS [*Kneeling*]
   Great Caesar—

CAESAR   Doth not Brutus bootless kneel?   76

CASCA   Speak, hands, for me!

        They stab Caesar, [Casca first, Brutus last].

CAESAR   *Et tu, Brutè?* Then fall, Caesar!   *Dies.* 78

CINNA
   Liberty! Freedom! Tyranny is dead!
   Run hence, proclaim, cry it about the streets.

CASSIUS
   Some to the common pulpits, and cry out   81
   "Liberty, freedom, and enfranchisement!"

BRUTUS
   People and senators, be not affrighted.
   Fly not; stand still. Ambition's debt is paid.   84

CASCA
   Go to the pulpit, Brutus.

DECIUS   And Cassius too.

BRUTUS   Where's Publius?   86

CINNA
   Here, quite confounded with this mutiny.   87

METELLUS
   Stand fast together, lest some friend of Caesar's
   Should chance—

BRUTUS
   Talk not of standing.—Publius, good cheer.   90

---

70 rank place in line or file, position   **71 Unshaked of motion** (1) unswayed by petitions (2) with perfectly steady movement   **75 Olympus** mountain dwelling of the Greek gods   **76 bootless** in vain   **78 Et tu, Brutè** and thou, Brutus   **81 common pulpits** public platforms or rostra   **84 Ambition's debt** what Caesar's ambition deserved **86 Publius** (An old senator, too confused to flee.)   **87 mutiny** uprising **90 standing** resistance

There is no harm intended to your person,
Nor to no Roman else. So tell them, Publius.

CASSIUS
And leave us, Publius, lest that the people,
Rushing on us, should do your age some mischief.

BRUTUS
Do so, and let no man abide this deed   95
But we the doers.   [*Exeunt all but the conspirators.*]

     Enter Trebonius.

CASSIUS
Where is Antony?

TREBONIUS   Fled to his house amazed.   97
Men, wives, and children stare, cry out, and run
As it were doomsday.

BRUTUS   Fates, we will know your pleasures.   99
That we shall die, we know; 'tis but the time,
And drawing days out, that men stand upon.   101

CASCA
Why, he that cuts off twenty years of life
Cuts off so many years of fearing death.

BRUTUS
Grant that, and then is death a benefit.
So are we Caesar's friends, that have abridged
His time of fearing death. Stoop, Romans, stoop,
And let us bathe our hands in Caesar's blood
Up to the elbows and besmear our swords.
Then walk we forth even to the marketplace,   109
And, waving our red weapons o'er our heads,
Let's all cry "Peace, freedom, and liberty!"

CASSIUS
Stoop, then, and wash. [*They bathe their hands and
     weapons.*] How many ages hence
Shall this our lofty scene be acted over
In states unborn and accents yet unknown!   114

BRUTUS
How many times shall Caesar bleed in sport,   115

95 abide (1) stand the consequences of (2) remain here with   **97 amazed**
stunned   **99 As** as if   **101 drawing . . . upon** prolonging their lives, that
men attach importance to   **109 the marketplace** i.e., the Forum
114 accents languages   **115 in sport** for entertainment

That now on Pompey's basis lies along   116
No worthier than the dust!
CASSIUS   So oft as that shall be,
So often shall the knot of us be called   119
The men that gave their country liberty.
DECIUS
What, shall we forth?
CASSIUS   Ay, every man away.
Brutus shall lead, and we will grace his heels   122
With the most boldest and best hearts of Rome.

    Enter a Servant.

BRUTUS
Soft, who comes here? A friend of Antony's.
SERVANT [*Kneeling*]
Thus, Brutus, did my master bid me kneel;
Thus did Mark Antony bid me fall down,
And being prostrate, thus he bade me say:
"Brutus is noble, wise, valiant, and honest;
Caesar was mighty, bold, royal, and loving.
Say I love Brutus and I honor him;
Say I feared Caesar, honored him, and loved him.
If Brutus will vouchsafe that Antony   132
May safely come to him and be resolved   133
How Caesar hath deserved to lie in death,
Mark Antony shall not love Caesar dead
So well as Brutus living, but will follow
The fortunes and affairs of noble Brutus
Thorough the hazards of this untrod state   138
With all true faith." So says my master Antony.
BRUTUS
Thy master is a wise and valiant Roman;
I never thought him worse.
Tell him, so please him come unto this place,   142
He shall be satisfied and, by my honor,
Depart untouched.

116 Pompey's basis pedestal of Pompey's statue.   **along** prostrate, at full
length   **119 knot** group   **122 grace** do honor to (by following closely)
132 vouchsafe allow   **133 be resolved** receive an explanation
138 Thorough through.   **untrod state** new state of affairs   **142 so** if it
should

SERVANT   I'll fetch him presently.   144

                               Exit Servant.

BRUTUS
I know that we shall have him well to friend.   145

CASSIUS
I wish we may. But yet have I a mind
That fears him much, and my misgiving still   147
Falls shrewdly to the purpose.   148

    Enter Antony.

BRUTUS
But here comes Antony.—Welcome, Mark Antony.

ANTONY
O mighty Caesar! Dost thou lie so low?
Are all thy conquests, glories, triumphs, spoils,
Shrunk to this little measure? Fare thee well.—
I know not, gentlemen, what you intend,
Who else must be let blood, who else is rank;   154
If I myself, there is no hour so fit
As Caesar's death's hour, nor no instrument
Of half that worth as those your swords, made rich
With the most noble blood of all this world.
I do beseech ye, if you bear me hard,   159
Now, whilst your purpled hands do reek and smoke,   160
Fulfill your pleasure. Live a thousand years,   161
I shall not find myself so apt to die;   162
No place will please me so, no means of death,
As here by Caesar, and by you cut off,
The choice and master spirits of this age.

BRUTUS
O Antony! Beg not your death of us.
Though now we must appear bloody and cruel,
As by our hands and this our present act
You see we do, yet see you but our hands

---

144 presently immediately   **145 to friend** for a friend   **147 fears** distrusts.
my misgiving still i.e., such misgiving on my part always or generally
148 Falls . . . purpose falls ominously close to the mark   **154 let blood** bled,
i.e., killed.   **rank** diseased and in need of bleeding (with pun on "overgrown,
too powerful")   **159 bear me hard** bear ill will to me   **160 purpled** bloody.
reek steam   **161 Live** if I should live   **162 apt** ready

And this the bleeding business they have done.
Our hearts you see not. They are pitiful; 171
And pity to the general wrong of Rome—
As fire drives out fire, so pity pity— 173
Hath done this deed on Caesar. For your part,
To you our swords have leaden points, Mark Antony. 175
Our arms in strength of malice, and our hearts 176
Of brothers' temper, do receive you in 177
With all kind love, good thoughts, and reverence.

CASSIUS
Your voice shall be as strong as any man's 179
In the disposing of new dignities. 180

BRUTUS
Only be patient till we have appeased
The multitude, beside themselves with fear,
And then we will deliver you the cause 183
Why I, that did love Caesar when I struck him,
Have thus proceeded.

ANTONY   I doubt not of your wisdom.
Let each man render me his bloody hand.
     [He shakes hands with the conspirators]
First, Marcus Brutus, will I shake with you;
Next, Caius Cassius, do I take your hand;
Now, Decius Brutus, yours; now yours, Metellus;
Yours, Cinna; and, my valiant Casca, yours;
Though last, not least in love, yours, good Trebonius.
Gentlemen all—alas, what shall I say?
My credit now stands on such slippery ground 193
That one of two bad ways you must conceit me, 194
Either a coward or a flatterer.
That I did love thee, Caesar, O, 'tis true!
If then thy spirit look upon us now,
Shall it not grieve thee dearer than thy death 198
To see thy Antony making his peace,
Shaking the bloody fingers of thy foes—

---

171 pitiful full of pity   **173 pity pity** i.e., pity for the general wrong of
Rome drove out pity for Caesar   **175 leaden** i.e., blunt   **176–177 Our
. . . temper** i.e., both our arms, though seeming strong in enmity, and
our hearts, full of brotherly feeling   **179 voice** vote, authority
180 dignities offices of state   **183 deliver** report to   **193 credit** credibil-
ity   **194 conceit** think, judge   **198 dearer** more deeply

Most noble!—in the presence of thy corpse?
Had I as many eyes as thou hast wounds,
Weeping as fast as they stream forth thy blood,
It would become me better than to close   204
In terms of friendship with thine enemies.
Pardon me, Julius! Here wast thou bayed, brave hart,   206
Here didst thou fall, and here thy hunters stand,
Signed in thy spoil and crimsoned in thy lethe.   208
O world, thou wast the forest to this hart,
And this indeed, O world, the heart of thee!
How like a deer, strucken by many princes,
Dost thou here lie!

CASSIUS
   Mark Antony—
ANTONY   Pardon me, Caius Cassius.
   The enemies of Caesar shall say this;   214
   Then in a friend it is cold modesty.   215

CASSIUS
   I blame you not for praising Caesar so,
   But what compact mean you to have with us?   217
   Will you be pricked in number of our friends, 218
   Or shall we on and not depend on you?

ANTONY
   Therefore I took your hands, but was indeed
   Swayed from the point by looking down on Caesar.
   Friends am I with you all, and love you all,
   Upon this hope, that you shall give me reasons
   Why and wherein Caesar was dangerous.

BRUTUS
   Or else were this a savage spectacle.   225
   Our reasons are so full of good regard   226
   That were you, Antony, the son of Caesar,
   You should be satisfied.
ANTONY   That's all I seek,

204 close come to an agreement   **206 bayed** brought to bay.   **hart** stag
(with pun on *heart*)   **208 Signed . . . spoil** marked with the tokens of
your slaughter.   **lethe** river of oblivion in the underworld, here associ-
ated with death and blood (perhaps fused with Cocytus, river of blood
in the underworld)   **214 The enemies** even the enemies   **215 cold**
sober.   **modesty** moderation   **217 compact** agreement   **218 pricked in
number** marked off on a list   **225 else were this** otherwise this would
be   **226 regard** account, consideration

And am moreover suitor that I may
Produce his body to the marketplace,   230
And in the pulpit, as becomes a friend,   231
Speak in the order of his funeral.   232

BRUTUS
You shall, Mark Antony.

CASSIUS   Brutus, a word with you.
[*Aside to Brutus.*] You know not what you do. Do not
  consent
That Antony speak in his funeral.
Know you how much the people may be moved
By that which he will utter?

BRUTUS [*Aside to Cassius*]   By your pardon:
I will myself into the pulpit first
And show the reason of our Caesar's death.
What Antony shall speak, I will protest   240
He speaks by leave and by permission,
And that we are contented Caesar shall
Have all true rites and lawful ceremonies.
It shall advantage more than do us wrong.

CASSIUS [*Aside to Brutus*]
I know not what may fall. I like it not.   245

BRUTUS
Mark Antony, here, take you Caesar's body.
You shall not in your funeral speech blame us,
But speak all good you can devise of Caesar,
And say you do 't by our permission.
Else shall you not have any hand at all
About his funeral. And you shall speak
In the same pulpit whereto I am going,
After my speech is ended.

ANTONY   Be it so.
I do desire no more.

BRUTUS
Prepare the body then, and follow us.   255
                        Exeunt. Manet Antony.

ANTONY
O, pardon me, thou bleeding piece of earth,

230 Produce bring forth **231 pulpit** public platform **232 order** ceremony **240 protest** announce **245 fall** befall, happen **255 s.d. Manet**
he remains onstage

That I am meek and gentle with these butchers!
Thou art the ruins of the noblest man
That ever livèd in the tide of times.   259
Woe to the hand that shed this costly blood!   260
Over thy wounds now do I prophesy—
Which, like dumb mouths, do ope their ruby lips
To beg the voice and utterance of my tongue—
A curse shall light upon the limbs of men;
Domestic fury and fierce civil strife
Shall cumber all the parts of Italy;   266
Blood and destruction shall be so in use
And dreadful objects so familiar   268
That mothers shall but smile when they behold
Their infants quartered with the hands of war,   270
All pity choked with custom of fell deeds;   271
And Caesar's spirit, ranging for revenge,   272
With Ate by his side come hot from hell,   273
Shall in these confines with a monarch's voice   274
Cry "Havoc!" and let slip the dogs of war,   275
That this foul deed shall smell above the earth   276
With carrion men, groaning for burial.

    Enter Octavius' Servant.

You serve Octavius Caesar, do you not?
SERVANT   I do, Mark Antony.
ANTONY
Caesar did write for him to come to Rome.
SERVANT
He did receive his letters, and is coming,
And bid me say to you by word of mouth—
O Caesar!   [*Seeing the body.*]
ANTONY
Thy heart is big. Get thee apart and weep.   284
Passion, I see, is catching, for mine eyes,

---

259 tide of times course of all history   **260 costly** (1) valuable (2) fraught
with dire consequences   **266 cumber** entangle   **268 objects** sights
270 quartered cut to pieces   **271 custom . . . deeds** the familiarity of
cruel deeds   **272 ranging** roaming up and down in search of prey
273 Ate goddess of discord and moral chaos   **274 confines** regions
275 Havoc (The signal for sack, pillage, and slaughter.)   **let slip**
unleash   **276 That** so that   **284 big** swollen with grief

Seeing those beads of sorrow stand in thine,
Began to water. Is thy master coming?

SERVANT

He lies tonight within seven leagues of Rome.   288

ANTONY

Post back with speed and tell him what hath chanced.
Here is a mourning Rome, a dangerous Rome,
No Rome of safety for Octavius yet;
Hie hence and tell him so. Yet stay awhile;   292
Thou shalt not back till I have borne this corpse
Into the marketplace. There shall I try,   294
In my oration, how the people take
The cruel issue of these bloody men,   296
According to the which thou shalt discourse   297
To young Octavius of the state of things.   298
Lend me your hand.   *Exeunt [with Caesar's body].*

✽

3.2   *Enter Brutus and [presently] goes into the
pulpit, and Cassius, with the Plebeians.*

PLEBEIANS

We will be satisfied! Let us be satisfied!   1

BRUTUS

Then follow me, and give me audience, friends.
Cassius, go you into the other street
And part the numbers.   4
Those that will hear me speak, let 'em stay here;
Those that will follow Cassius, go with him;
And public reasons shall be renderèd
Of Caesar's death.
FIRST PLEBEIAN   I will hear Brutus speak.
SECOND PLEBEIAN

I will hear Cassius, and compare their reasons
When severally we hear them renderèd.   10
          [Exit Cassius, with some of the Plebeians.]

288 seven leagues about 20 miles   **292 Hie** hasten   **294 try** test
296 issue deed   **297 the which** the outcome of which   **298 young
Octavius** (He was eighteen in March of 44 B.C.)

3.2. Location: The Forum.
1 be satisfied have an explanation   **4 part** divide   **10 severally** individually, separately

THIRD PLEBEIAN
  The noble Brutus is ascended. Silence!
BRUTUS   Be patient till the last.
  Romans, countrymen, and lovers, hear me for my 13
cause, and be silent that you may hear. Believe me for
mine honor, and have respect to mine honor, that you
may believe. Censure me in your wisdom, and awake 16
your senses, that you may the better judge. If there be 17
any in this assembly, any dear friend of Caesar's, to
him I say that Brutus' love to Caesar was no less than
his. If then that friend demand why Brutus rose
against Caesar, this is my answer: not that I loved Caesar less, but that I loved Rome more. Had you rather
Caesar were living and die all slaves, than that Caesar
were dead, to live all free men? As Caesar loved me, I
weep for him; as he was fortunate, I rejoice at it; as he
was valiant, I honor him; but, as he was ambitious, I
slew him. There is tears for his love; joy for his fortune; honor for his valor; and death for his ambition.
Who is here so base that would be a bondman? If any,
speak, for him have I offended. Who is here so rude 30
that would not be a Roman? If any, speak, for him
have I offended. Who is here so vile that will not love
his country? If any, speak, for him have I offended. I
pause for a reply.
ALL   None, Brutus, none!
BRUTUS   Then none have I offended. I have done no
more to Caesar than you shall do to Brutus. The ques- 37
tion of his death is enrolled in the Capitol, his glory 38
not extenuated wherein he was worthy, nor his 39
offenses enforced for which he suffered death.   40

      *Enter Mark Antony [and others] with Caesar's
      body.*

13 **lovers** friends. (This speech by Brutus is in what Plutarch calls the
Lacedemonian or Spartan style, brief and sententious. Its content is
original with Shakespeare.)   16 **Censure** judge   17 **senses** intellectual
powers   30 **rude** barbarous   37 **shall** i.e., should, if I were to do as
Caesar did   37–38 **The question . . . enrolled** the considerations that
necessitated his death are recorded   39 **extenuated** minimized
40 **enforced** exaggerated, insisted upon

Here comes his body, mourned by Mark Antony, who,
though he had no hand in his death, shall receive the
benefit of his dying, a place in the commonwealth, as
which of you shall not? With this I depart, that, as I
slew my best lover for the good of Rome, I have the 45
same dagger for myself when it shall please my country to need my death.

ALL Live, Brutus, live, live!

> [*Brutus comes down.*]

FIRST PLEBEIAN
Bring him with triumph home unto his house.

SECOND PLEBEIAN
Give him a statue with his ancestors.   50

THIRD PLEBEIAN
Let him be Caesar.

FOURTH PLEBEIAN   Caesar's better parts
Shall be crowned in Brutus.

FIRST PLEBEIAN
We'll bring him to his house with shouts and clamors.

BRUTUS
My countrymen—

SECOND PLEBEIAN ' Peace, silence! Brutus speaks.

FIRST PLEBEIAN Peace, ho!

BRUTUS
Good countrymen, let me depart alone,
And, for my sake, stay here with Antony.
Do grace to Caesar's corpse, and grace his speech   58
Tending to Caesar's glories, which Mark Antony,   59
By our permission, is allowed to make.
I do entreat you, not a man depart,
Save I alone, till Antony have spoke.   *Exit.*

FIRST PLEBEIAN
Stay, ho, and let us hear Mark Antony.

THIRD PLEBEIAN
Let him go up into the public chair.
We'll hear him. Noble Antony, go up.

---

45 lover friend   **50 Second Plebeian** (Not the same person who exited at
l. 10; the numbering here refers to those who stay to hear Brutus.)
58 Do grace show respect.   **grace his speech** i.e., listen courteously to
Antony's speech   **59 Tending to** relating to, dealing with

ANTONY
  For Brutus' sake I am beholding to you.   66
                         [*He goes into the pulpit.*]
FOURTH PLEBEIAN   What does he say of Brutus?
THIRD PLEBEIAN   He says, for Brutus' sake
  He finds himself beholding to us all.
FOURTH PLEBEIAN
  'Twere best he speak no harm of Brutus here.
FIRST PLEBEIAN
  This Caesar was a tyrant.
THIRD PLEBEIAN   Nay, that's certain.
  We are blest that Rome is rid of him.
SECOND PLEBEIAN
  Peace! Let us hear what Antony can say.
ANTONY
  You gentle Romans—
ALL   Peace, ho! Let us hear him.
ANTONY
  Friends, Romans, countrymen, lend me your ears.   75
  I come to bury Caesar, not to praise him.
  The evil that men do lives after them;
  The good is oft interrèd with their bones.
  So let it be with Caesar. The noble Brutus
  Hath told you Caesar was ambitious.
  If it were so, it was a grievous fault,
  And grievously hath Caesar answered it.   82
  Here, under leave of Brutus and the rest—   83
  For Brutus is an honorable man,
  So are they all, all honorable men—
  Come I to speak in Caesar's funeral.
  He was my friend, faithful and just to me;
  But Brutus says he was ambitious,
  And Brutus is an honorable man.
  He hath brought many captives home to Rome,
  Whose ransoms did the general coffers fill.
  Did this in Caesar seem ambitious?
  When that the poor have cried, Caesar hath wept;

66 beholding beholden   **75 Friends** (This speech by Antony is thought to
illustrate the Asiatic or "florid" style of speaking. In it Shakespeare
gathers various hints from Plutarch, Appian, and Dion, but the speech
is Shakespeare's invention.)   **82 answered** paid the penalty for
83 under leave by permission

Ambition should be made of sterner stuff.
Yet Brutus says he was ambitious,
And Brutus is an honorable man.
You all did see that on the Lupercal   97
I thrice presented him a kingly crown,
Which he did thrice refuse. Was this ambition?
Yet Brutus says he was ambitious,
And sure he is an honorable man.
I speak not to disprove what Brutus spoke,
But here I am to speak what I do know.
You all did love him once, not without cause.
What cause withholds you then to mourn for him?
O judgment! Thou art fled to brutish beasts,
And men have lost their reason. Bear with me;
My heart is in the coffin there with Caesar,
And I must pause till it come back to me.

FIRST PLEBEIAN
Methinks there is much reason in his sayings.

SECOND PLEBEIAN
If thou consider rightly of the matter,
Caesar has had great wrong.

THIRD PLEBEIAN   Has he, masters?
I fear there will a worse come in his place.

FOURTH PLEBEIAN
Marked ye his words? He would not take the crown,
Therefore 'tis certain he was not ambitious.

FIRST PLEBEIAN
If it be found so, some will dear abide it.   116

SECOND PLEBEIAN
Poor soul, his eyes are red as fire with weeping.

THIRD PLEBEIAN
There's not a nobler man in Rome than Antony.

FOURTH PLEBEIAN
Now mark him. He begins again to speak.

ANTONY
But yesterday the word of Caesar might
Have stood against the world. Now lies he there,
And none so poor to do him reverence.   122

---

97 Lupercal (See 1.1.67 and note.)   **116 dear abide it** pay a heavy penalty for it   **122 none . . . reverence** i.e., no one, not even the lowliest
person, is below Caesar in fortune now, making obeisance to him

O masters! If I were disposed to stir
Your hearts and minds to mutiny and rage,   124
I should do Brutus wrong, and Cassius wrong,
Who, you all know, are honorable men.
I will not do them wrong; I rather choose
To wrong the dead, to wrong myself and you,
Than I will wrong such honorable men.
But here's a parchment with the seal of Caesar.
I found it in his closet; 'tis his will.   131
                              [*He shows the will.*]
Let but the commons hear this testament—   132
Which, pardon me, I do not mean to read—
And they would go and kiss dead Caesar's wounds
And dip their napkins in his sacred blood,   135
Yea, beg a hair of him for memory,
And dying, mention it within their wills,
Bequeathing it as a rich legacy
Unto their issue.

FOURTH PLEBEIAN
We'll hear the will! Read it, Mark Antony.

ALL
The will, the will! We will hear Caesar's will.

ANTONY
Have patience, gentle friends; I must not read it.
It is not meet you know how Caesar loved you.   143
You are not wood, you are not stones, but men;
And being men, hearing the will of Caesar,
It will inflame you, it will make you mad.
'Tis good you know not that you are his heirs,
For if you should, O, what would come of it?

FOURTH PLEBEIAN
Read the will! We'll hear it, Antony.
You shall read us the will, Caesar's will.

ANTONY
Will you be patient? Will you stay awhile?
I have o'ershot myself to tell you of it.   152
I fear I wrong the honorable men
Whose daggers have stabbed Caesar; I do fear it.

---

124 mutiny riot, tumult   **131 closet** private chamber   **132 commons**
common people   **135 napkins** handkerchiefs   **143 meet** fitting that
152 o'ershot myself gone further than I should

FOURTH PLEBEIAN
  They were traitors. "Honorable men"!
ALL   The will! The testament!
SECOND PLEBEIAN
  They were villains, murderers. The will! Read the will!
ANTONY
  You will compel me then to read the will?
  Then make a ring about the corpse of Caesar
  And let me show you him that made the will.
  Shall I descend? And will you give me leave?
ALL   Come down.
SECOND PLEBEIAN   Descend.
THIRD PLEBEIAN   You shall have leave.
      [*Antony comes down. They gather around Caesar.*]
FOURTH PLEBEIAN   A ring; stand round.
FIRST PLEBEIAN
  Stand from the hearse. Stand from the body.   166
SECOND PLEBEIAN
  Room for Antony, most noble Antony!
ANTONY
  Nay, press not so upon me. Stand far off.   168
ALL   Stand back! Room! Bear back!
ANTONY
  If you have tears, prepare to shed them now.
  You all do know this mantle. I remember   171
  The first time ever Caesar put it on;
  'Twas on a summer's evening in his tent,
  That day he overcame the Nervii.   174
  Look, in this place ran Cassius' dagger through.
  See what a rent the envious Casca made.   176
  Through this the well-belovèd Brutus stabbed,
  And as he plucked his cursèd steel away,
  Mark how the blood of Caesar followed it,
  As rushing out of doors to be resolved   180
  If Brutus so unkindly knocked or no;   181
  For Brutus, as you know, was Caesar's angel.   182
  Judge, O you gods, how dearly Caesar loved him!

166 hearse bier   **168 far** farther   **171 mantle** cloak, toga   **174 the
Nervii** the Belgian tribe whose defeat in 57 B.C. is described in Caesar's
Gallic War, 2.15–28   **176 rent** tear, hole.   **envious** malicious, spiteful
180 be resolved learn for certain   **181 unkindly** cruelly and unnatu-
rally   **182 angel** i.e., daimon or genius, second self

This was the most unkindest cut of all;   184
For when the noble Caesar saw him stab,
Ingratitude, more strong than traitors' arms,
Quite vanquished him. Then burst his mighty heart,
And in his mantle muffling up his face,
Even at the base of Pompey's statue,
Which all the while ran blood, great Caesar fell.
O, what a fall was there, my countrymen!
Then I, and you, and all of us fell down,
Whilst bloody treason flourished over us.   193
O, now you weep, and I perceive you feel
The dint of pity. These are gracious drops.   195
Kind souls, what weep you when you but behold   196
Our Caesar's vesture wounded? Look you here,   197
Here is himself, marred as you see with traitors.

                              [*He lifts Caesar's mantle.*]

FIRST PLEBEIAN   O piteous spectacle!
SECOND PLEBEIAN   O noble Caesar!
THIRD PLEBEIAN   O woeful day!
FOURTH PLEBEIAN   O traitors, villains!
FIRST PLEBEIAN   O most bloody sight!
SECOND PLEBEIAN   We will be revenged.
ALL   Revenge! About! Seek! Burn! Fire! Kill! Slay! Let 205
not a traitor live!
ANTONY   Stay, countrymen.
FIRST PLEBEIAN   Peace there! Hear the noble Antony.
SECOND PLEBEIAN   We'll hear him, we'll follow him,
we'll die with him!
ANTONY
Good friends, sweet friends, let me not stir you up
To such a sudden flood of mutiny.
They that have done this deed are honorable.
What private griefs they have, alas, I know not,   214
That made them do it. They are wise and honorable,
And will no doubt with reasons answer you.
I come not, friends, to steal away your hearts.

---

184 unkindest (1) most cruel (2) most unnatural. (The double superlative
was grammatically acceptable in Shakespeare's day.)   **193 flourished**
triumphed insolently   **195 dint** impression   **196 what** why
197 vesture garment   **205 About** to work   **214 griefs** grievances

I am no orator, as Brutus is,
But, as you know me all, a plain blunt man
That love my friend, and that they know full well
That gave me public leave to speak of him.   221
For I have neither wit, nor words, nor worth,   222
Action, nor utterance, nor the power of speech   223
To stir men's blood. I only speak right on.
I tell you that which you yourselves do know,
Show you sweet Caesar's wounds, poor poor dumb
    mouths,
And bid them speak for me. But were I Brutus,
And Brutus Antony, there were an Antony
Would ruffle up your spirits and put a tongue   229
In every wound of Caesar that should move
The stones of Rome to rise and mutiny.

ALL
We'll mutiny!
FIRST PLEBEIAN We'll burn the house of Brutus!
THIRD PLEBEIAN
Away, then! Come, seek the conspirators.
ANTONY
Yet hear me, countrymen. Yet hear me speak.
ALL
Peace, ho! Hear Antony, most noble Antony!
ANTONY
Why, friends, you go to do you know not what.
Wherein hath Caesar thus deserved your loves?
Alas, you know not. I must tell you then:
You have forgot the will I told you of.
ALL
Most true, the will! Let's stay and hear the will.
ANTONY
Here is the will, and under Caesar's seal.
To every Roman citizen he gives,
To every several man, seventy-five drachmas.   243
SECOND PLEBEIAN
Most noble Caesar! We'll revenge his death.

221 public leave permission to speak publicly   **222 wit** understanding,
intelligence.   **worth** stature, authority   **223 Action** gesture.   **utterance**
good delivery   **229 ruffle up** stir to anger   **243 several** individual.
drachmas coins. (This is a substantial bequest.)

THIRD PLEBEIAN   O royal Caesar!
ANTONY   Hear me with patience.
ALL   Peace, ho!
ANTONY
　　Moreover, he hath left you all his walks,
　　His private arbors, and new-planted orchards,   249
　　On this side Tiber; he hath left them you,
　　And to your heirs forever—common pleasures,   251
　　To walk abroad and recreate yourselves.
　　Here was a Caesar! When comes such another?
FIRST PLEBEIAN
　　Never, never! Come, away, away!
　　We'll burn his body in the holy place
　　And with the brands fire the traitors' houses.
　　Take up the body.
SECOND PLEBEIAN   Go fetch fire!
THIRD PLEBEIAN   Pluck down benches!
FOURTH PLEBEIAN   Pluck down forms, windows, anything! 260
　　　　　　　　Exeunt Plebeians [with the body].
ANTONY
　　Now let it work. Mischief, thou art afoot.
　　Take thou what course thou wilt.

　　　　　Enter Servant.

　　　　　　　　　　　　How now, fellow?
SERVANT
　　Sir, Octavius is already come to Rome.
ANTONY   Where is he?
SERVANT
　　He and Lepidus are at Caesar's house.
ANTONY
　　And thither will I straight to visit him.   266
　　He comes upon a wish. Fortune is merry,   267
　　And in this mood will give us anything.
SERVANT
　　I heard him say Brutus and Cassius
　　Are rid like madmen through the gates of Rome.   270

---

249 orchards gardens   **251 common pleasures** public pleasure gardens
(in which)   **260 forms** benches.   **windows** i.e., shutters   **266 straight**
straightway, at once   **267 upon a wish** just when wanted.   **merry** i.e.,
favorably disposed   **270 Are rid** have ridden

ANTONY

    Belike they had some notice of the people,   271
    How I had moved them. Bring me to Octavius.

                                   Exeunt.

                       ❖

3.3   *Enter Cinna the poet, and after him the*
           Plebeians.

CINNA

    I dreamt tonight that I did feast with Caesar,   1
    And things unluckily charge my fantasy.   2
    I have no will to wander forth of doors,
    Yet something leads me forth.

FIRST PLEBEIAN   What is your name?

SECOND PLEBEIAN   Whither are you going?

THIRD PLEBEIAN   Where do you dwell?

FOURTH PLEBEIAN   Are you a married man or a bachelor?

SECOND PLEBEIAN   Answer every man directly.

FIRST PLEBEIAN   Ay, and briefly.

FOURTH PLEBEIAN   Ay, and wisely.

THIRD PLEBEIAN   Ay, and truly, you were best.   13

CINNA   What is my name? Whither am I going? Where
    do I dwell? Am I a married man or a bachelor? Then
    to answer every man directly and briefly, wisely and
    truly: wisely I say, I am a bachelor.

SECOND PLEBEIAN   That's as much as to say they are
    fools that marry. You'll bear me a bang for that, I fear.   19
    Proceed directly.

CINNA   Directly, I am going to Caesar's funeral.

FIRST PLEBEIAN   As a friend or an enemy?

CINNA   As a friend.

SECOND PLEBEIAN   That matter is answered directly.

FOURTH PLEBEIAN   For your dwelling—briefly.

CINNA   Briefly, I dwell by the Capitol.

THIRD PLEBEIAN   Your name, sir, truly.

271 Belike likely enough. **of** about; or from

3.3. Location: A street.
1 tonight last night   **2 unluckily . . . fantasy** oppress my imagination
with foreboding   **13 you were best** it would be best for you   **19 bear
. . . bang** get a beating from me

CINNA   Truly, my name is Cinna.

FIRST PLEBEIAN   Tear him to pieces! He's a conspirator!

CINNA   I am Cinna the poet, I am Cinna the poet!

FOURTH PLEBEIAN   Tear him for his bad verses, tear him for his bad verses!

CINNA   I am not Cinna the conspirator.

FOURTH PLEBEIAN   It is no matter, his name's Cinna. Pluck but his name out of his heart, and turn him 35 going. 36

THIRD PLEBEIAN   Tear him, tear him! Come, brands, ho, firebrands! To Brutus', to Cassius'; burn all! Some to Decius' house, and some to Casca's; some to Ligarius'. Away, go!

        Exeunt all the Plebeians, [dragging off Cinna].

❖

35–36 turn him going send him packing

4.1   *Enter Antony [with a list], Octavius, and*
          Lepidus.

ANTONY
  These many, then, shall die. Their names are pricked.   1
OCTAVIUS
  Your brother too must die. Consent you, Lepidus?
LEPIDUS
  I do consent—
OCTAVIUS   Prick him down, Antony.
LEPIDUS
  Upon condition Publius shall not live,
  Who is your sister's son, Mark Antony.
ANTONY
  He shall not live. Look, with a spot I damn him.   6
  But Lepidus, go you to Caesar's house.
  Fetch the will hither, and we shall determine   8
  How to cut off some charge in legacies.   9
LEPIDUS   What, shall I find you here?
OCTAVIUS   Or here or at the Capitol.   *Exit Lepidus.*   11
ANTONY
  This is a slight unmeritable man,   12
  Meet to be sent on errands. Is it fit,
  The threefold world divided, he should stand   14
  One of the three to share it?
OCTAVIUS   So you thought him,
  And took his voice who should be pricked to die   16
  In our black sentence and proscription.   17
ANTONY
  Octavius, I have seen more days than you;
  And though we lay these honors on this man

4.1. Location: Rome. A table is perhaps set out.
1 pricked marked down on a list (appropriate to the use of the stylus on
waxen tablets or of a pin on paper)   **6 spot** mark (on the list).   **damn**
condemn   **8–9 determine . . . legacies** i.e., find a way to reduce the
outlay of Caesar's estate, by altering the will   **11 Or** either   **12 slight
unmeritable** insignificant and undeserving   **14 threefold** (i.e., including
Europe, Africa, and Asia; alluding also to the triumvirate of Lepidus,
Antony, Octavius)   **16 took his voice** allowed him to decide (i.e., about
Publius); or, asked his opinion   **17 proscription** (Proscription branded a
man as an outlaw, confiscated his property, offered a reward for his
murder, and forbade his sons and grandsons from holding public office.)

To ease ourselves of divers slanderous loads,   20
He shall but bear them as the ass bears gold,
To groan and sweat under the business,
Either led or driven as we point the way;
And having brought our treasure where we will,
Then take we down his load, and turn him off,
Like to the empty ass, to shake his ears   26
And graze in commons.
OCTAVIUS   You may do your will;   27
But he's a tried and valiant soldier.
ANTONY
So is my horse, Octavius, and for that
I do appoint him store of provender.   30
It is a creature that I teach to fight,
To wind, to stop, to run directly on,   32
His corporal motion governed by my spirit.   33
And in some taste is Lepidus but so.   34
He must be taught, and trained, and bid go forth—
A barren-spirited fellow, one that feeds
On objects, arts, and imitations,   37
Which, out of use and staled by other men,   38
Begin his fashion. Do not talk of him   39
But as a property. And now, Octavius,   40
Listen great things. Brutus and Cassius   41
Are levying powers. We must straight make head.   42
Therefore let our alliance be combined,   43
Our best friends made, our means stretched;   44
And let us presently go sit in council   45
How covert matters may be best disclosed   46
And open perils surest answerèd.   47

20 divers . . . loads i.e., some of the burdensome accusations that will be
leveled against us   **26 empty** unloaded   **27 commons** public pasture
30 appoint assign, provide   **32 wind** turn. (Horse trainer's term.)
33 corporal bodily   **34 taste** degree, sense   **37 On . . . imitations** on
curiosities, artificial things, and the following of fashion (?), i.e., copied
things merely, taken up secondhand   **38 staled** made common or
cheap   **39 Begin his fashion** i.e., these outworn fashions are chosen by
him as his fashion   **40 property** tool   **41 Listen** hear   **42 powers**
armies.   **straight make head** immediately raise an army   **43 combined**
coalesced (i.e., let us work as one)   **44 made** mustered.   **stretched** used
to fullest advantage, extended to the utmost   **45 presently** at once
46 How . . . disclosed (to determine) how hidden dangers may best be
discovered   **47 surest answerèd** most safely met

OCTAVIUS

Let us do so, for we are at the stake   48
And bayed about with many enemies;   49
And some that smile have in their hearts, I fear,
Millions of mischiefs.   *Exeunt.* 51

✤

4.2   *Drum. Enter Brutus, Lucilius, [Lucius,] and the*
         army. Titinius and Pindarus meet them.

BRUTUS   Stand, ho!   1
LUCILIUS   Give the word, ho, and stand!   2
BRUTUS
What now, Lucilius, is Cassius near?
LUCILIUS
He is at hand, and Pindarus is come
To do you salutation from his master.
BRUTUS
He greets me well. Your master, Pindarus,   6
In his own change, or by ill officers,   7
Hath given me some worthy cause to wish
Things done, undone; but if he be at hand
I shall be satisfied.
PINDARUS   I do not doubt   10
But that my noble master will appear
Such as he is, full of regard and honor.   12
BRUTUS
He is not doubted.—A word, Lucilius.
              [Brutus and Lucilius speak apart.]
How he received you let me be resolved.   14
LUCILIUS
With courtesy and with respect enough,

---

48 at the stake i.e., like a bear in the sport of bearbaiting   **49 bayed
about** surrounded as by baying dogs   **51 mischiefs** harms, evils

**4.2. Location: Camp near Sardis, in Asia Minor. Before Brutus' tent.
1–2 Stand . . . stand** halt! Pass the word   **6 well** i.e., ceremoniously,
through Pindarus (who is only a slave; perhaps Brutus is ironic)   **7 In
. . . officers** whether from an alteration in his feelings toward me, or
through the acts of unworthy subordinates   **10 be satisfied** have things
explained to my satisfaction   **12 regard** i.e., consideration of your joint
interests   **14 resolved** informed, put out of doubt

But not with such familiar instances   16
Nor with such free and friendly conference   17
As he hath used of old.
BRUTUS   Thou hast described
A hot friend cooling. Ever note, Lucilius,
When love begins to sicken and decay
It useth an enforcèd ceremony.   21
There are no tricks in plain and simple faith.
But hollow men, like horses hot at hand,   23
Make gallant show and promise of their mettle;
                        Low march within
But when they should endure the bloody spur,
They fall their crests and like deceitful jades   26
Sink in the trial. Comes his army on?   27
LUCILIUS
They mean this night in Sardis to be quartered.   28
The greater part, the horse in general,   29
Are come with Cassius.

    Enter Cassius and his powers.

BRUTUS   Hark, he is arrived.
March gently on to meet him.   31
CASSIUS   Stand, ho!
BRUTUS   Stand, ho! Speak the word along.
FIRST SOLDIER   Stand!
SECOND SOLDIER   Stand!
THIRD SOLDIER   Stand!
CASSIUS
Most noble brother, you have done me wrong.
BRUTUS
Judge me, you gods! Wrong I mine enemies?
And if not so, how should I wrong a brother?
CASSIUS
Brutus, this sober form of yours hides wrongs;   40

16 familiar instances proofs of intimate friendship   **17 conference**
conversation   **21 enforcèd** constrained   **23 hollow** insincere.   **hot at
hand** restless and full of spirit when held in, at the start   **26 fall their
crests** lower their necks, hang their heads.   **jades** worthless horses
27 Sink give way, fail   **28 Sardis** (The capital city of Lydia in Asia
Minor.)   **29 the horse in general** all the cavalry   **31 gently** mildly, not
hostilely   **40 sober form** dignified manner

And when you do them—
BRUTUS   Cassius, be content;
   Speak your griefs softly. I do know you well.   42
   Before the eyes of both our armies here,
   Which should perceive nothing but love from us,
   Let us not wrangle. Bid them move away.
   Then in my tent, Cassius, enlarge your griefs,   46
   And I will give you audience.
CASSIUS   Pindarus,
   Bid our commanders lead their charges off   48
   A little from this ground.
BRUTUS
   Lucius, do you the like, and let no man
   Come to our tent till we have done our conference.
   Let Lucilius and Titinius guard our door.   52
       Exeunt. Manent Brutus and Cassius. [Lucilius
               and Titinius stand guard at the door.]

4.3

CASSIUS
   That you have wronged me doth appear in this:
   You have condemned and noted Lucius Pella   2
   For taking bribes here of the Sardians,
   Wherein my letters, praying on his side,   4
   Because I knew the man, was slighted off.   5
BRUTUS
   You wronged yourself to write in such a case.
CASSIUS
   In such a time as this it is not meet   7
   That every nice offense should bear his comment.   8

---

42 griefs grievances   **46 enlarge** speak freely   **48 charges** troops
52 Lucilius (The Folio reads *Lucius* here and *Lucilius* in l. 50, but when
Shakespeare interpolated a passage in the next scene at ll. 124–166 he
evidently intended to have Lucilius guarding the door.)

**4.3. Location: The scene is continuous. Brutus and Cassius remain on-
stage, which now represents the interior of Brutus' tent.**
2 noted publicly disgraced.   **Lucius Pella** a Roman praetor in Sardis
4 letters i.e., letter   **5 slighted off** slightingly dismissed   **7 meet** fitting   **8 nice** trivial.   **bear his comment** be made the object of scrutiny

BRUTUS
  Let me tell you, Cassius, you yourself
  Are much condemned to have an itching palm,   10
  To sell and mart your offices for gold   11
  To undeservers.

CASSIUS   I an itching palm?
  You know that you are Brutus that speaks this,
  Or, by the gods, this speech were else your last.   14

BRUTUS
  The name of Cassius honors this corruption,   15
  And chastisement doth therefore hide his head.   16

CASSIUS   Chastisement?

BRUTUS
  Remember March, the ides of March remember.
  Did not great Julius bleed for justice' sake?
  What villain touched his body that did stab
  And not for justice? What, shall one of us,
  That struck the foremost man of all this world
  But for supporting robbers, shall we now   23
  Contaminate our fingers with base bribes,
  And sell the mighty space of our large honors   25
  For so much trash as may be graspèd thus?   26
  I had rather be a dog and bay the moon   27
  Than such a Roman.

CASSIUS   Brutus, bait not me.   28
  I'll not endure it. You forget yourself
  To hedge me in. I am a soldier, I,   30
  Older in practice, abler than yourself
  To make conditions.   32

BRUTUS   Go to! You are not, Cassius.

CASSIUS   I am.

BRUTUS   I say you are not.

---

10 condemned to have accused of having   **11 mart** traffic in   **14 else** otherwise   **15 honors** lends the appearance of honor to, countenances   **16 chastisement . . . head** i.e., legal authority is afraid to act (because of Cassius' influence)   **23 But** only.   **robbers** i.e., those who would have robbed Rome of her liberty (?) (According to Plutarch, Caesar "was a favorer and suborner of all of them that did rob and spoil by his countenance and authority.")   **25 the mighty . . . honors** the greatness of our honorable reputations   **26 trash** i.e., money (despised in Brutus' stoic philosophy)   **27 bay** howl at   **28 bait** harass   **30 hedge me in** limit my authority   **32 make conditions** i.e., for the behavior of such men as Lucius Pella and for the appointment of my officers

CASSIUS
    Urge me no more; I shall forget myself.   36
    Have mind upon your health. Tempt me no farther.   37
BRUTUS   Away, slight man!   38
CASSIUS
    Is 't possible?
BRUTUS   Hear me, for I will speak.
    Must I give way and room to your rash choler?   40
    Shall I be frighted when a madman stares?   41
CASSIUS
    O ye gods, ye gods! Must I endure all this?
BRUTUS
    All this? Ay, more. Fret till your proud heart break.
    Go show your slaves how choleric you are
    And make your bondmen tremble. Must I budge?   45
    Must I observe you? Must I stand and crouch   46
    Under your testy humor? By the gods,
    You shall digest the venom of your spleen   48
    Though it do split you; for, from this day forth,
    I'll use you for my mirth, yea, for my laughter,
    When you are waspish.
CASSIUS   Is it come to this?   51
BRUTUS
    You say you are a better soldier.
    Let it appear so; make your vaunting true,   53
    And it shall please me well. For mine own part,
    I shall be glad to learn of noble men.   55
CASSIUS
    You wrong me every way! You wrong me, Brutus.
    I said an elder soldier, not a better.
    Did I say "better"?
BRUTUS   If you did, I care not.
CASSIUS
    When Caesar lived he durst not thus have moved me.   59
BRUTUS
    Peace, peace! You durst not so have tempted him.   60

36 **Urge** provoke 37 **Tempt** provoke 38 **slight** insignificant 40 **give
way and room to** make allowance for and accept. **choler** wrathful
temperament 41 **stares** looks wildly at me 45 **budge** flinch
46 **observe** pay reverence to. **crouch** bow, cringe 48 **digest** swallow.
spleen i.e., irascibility 51 **waspish** hotheaded 53 **vaunting** boasting
55 **learn of** learn of the existence of; or, learn from (those who have
proved themselves noble) 59 **moved** angered 60 **tempted** provoked

CASSIUS I durst not?

BRUTUS   No.

CASSIUS

What, durst not tempt him?

BRUTUS   For your life you durst not.

CASSIUS

Do not presume too much upon my love.
I may do that I shall be sorry for.

BRUTUS

You have done that you should be sorry for.
There is no terror, Cassius, in your threats,
For I am armed so strong in honesty
That they pass by me as the idle wind,
Which I respect not. I did send to you   70
For certain sums of gold, which you denied me;
For I can raise no money by vile means.
By heaven, I had rather coin my heart
And drop my blood for drachmas than to wring
From the hard hands of peasants their vile trash
By any indirection. I did send   76
To you for gold to pay my legions,
Which you denied me. Was that done like Cassius?
Should I have answered Caius Cassius so?
When Marcus Brutus grows so covetous
To lock such rascal counters from his friends,   81
Be ready, gods, with all your thunderbolts;
Dash him to pieces!

CASSIUS   I denied you not.

BRUTUS

You did.

CASSIUS   I did not. He was but a fool
That brought my answer back. Brutus hath rived my
    heart.   85
A friend should bear his friend's infirmities,
But Brutus makes mine greater than they are.

BRUTUS

I do not, till you practice them on me.

---

70 respect not pay no attention to **76 indirection** devious or unjust
means **81 rascal counters** i.e., paltry sums. (*Counters* were uncurrent
coins used by shopkeepers as discs in making reckonings.) **85 rived**
cleft, split

CASSIUS
You love me not.
BRUTUS   I do not like your faults.
CASSIUS
A friendly eye could never see such faults.
BRUTUS
A flatterer's would not, though they do appear
As huge as high Olympus.
CASSIUS
Come, Antony, and young Octavius, come,
Revenge yourselves alone on Cassius,
For Cassius is aweary of the world;
Hated by one he loves, braved by his brother,   96
Checked like a bondman, all his faults observed,   97
Set in a notebook, learned and conned by rote   98
To cast into my teeth. O, I could weep
My spirit from mine eyes! There is my dagger,
                    [*He offers his unsheathed dagger*]
And here my naked breast; within, a heart
Dearer than Pluto's mine, richer than gold   102
If that thou be'st a Roman, take it forth.
I, that denied thee gold, will give my heart.   104
Strike, as thou didst at Caesar; for I know,
When thou didst hate him worst, thou lovedst him better
Than ever thou lovedst Cassius.
BRUTUS   Sheathe your dagger.
Be angry when you will, it shall have scope;   108
Do what you will, dishonor shall be humor.   109
O Cassius, you are yokèd with a lamb   110
That carries anger as the flint bears fire,
Who, much enforcèd, shows a hasty spark   112
And straight is cold again.
CASSIUS   Hath Cassius lived   113
To be but mirth and laughter to his Brutus
When grief and blood ill-tempered vexeth him?   115

96 **braved** defied   97 **Checked** rebuked   98 **conned by rote** memorized
102 **Dearer** more laden with wealth.   **Pluto** god of the underworld (confused with Plutus, god of riches)   104 **that denied** i.e., who you insist
denied   108 **scope** free rein   109 **dishonor . . . humor** i.e., I'll regard your
corruption or your flaring temper as something to be humored   110 **yokèd
with** allied with (i.e., Brutus compares himself to the lamb)   112 **enforcèd**
provoked, struck upon   113 **straight** at once   115 **blood ill-tempered** i.e.,
disposition imbalanced by the humors of the body

BRUTUS
When I spoke that, I was ill-tempered too.

CASSIUS
Do you confess so much? Give me your hand.

BRUTUS
And my heart too.   [*They embrace.*]

CASSIUS   O Brutus!

BRUTUS   What's the matter?

CASSIUS
Have not you love enough to bear with me,
When that rash humor which my mother gave me   120
Makes me forgetful?

BRUTUS   Yes, Cassius, and from henceforth,
When you are overearnest with your Brutus,
He'll think your mother chides, and leave you so.   123

*Enter a Poet [followed by Lucilius and Titinius,
who have been standing guard at the door].*

POET
Let me go in to see the generals!
There is some grudge between 'em; 'tis not meet
They be alone.

LUCILIUS   You shall not come to them.

POET   Nothing but death shall stay me.

CASSIUS   How now? What's the matter?

POET
For shame, you generals! What do you mean?
Love and be friends, as two such men should be;
For I have seen more years, I'm sure, than ye.

CASSIUS
Ha, ha, how vilely doth this cynic rhyme!   132

BRUTUS
Get you hence, sirrah. Saucy fellow, hence!

CASSIUS
Bear with him, Brutus. 'Tis his fashion.

BRUTUS
I'll know his humor when he knows his time.   135

---

120 that rash humor i.e., choler, anger   **123 leave you so** let it go at
that   **132 cynic** i.e., rude fellow; also one claiming to be a Cynic philosopher, hence outspoken against luxury   **135 I'll . . . time** I'll indulge his
eccentric behavior when he knows the proper time for it

What should the wars do with these jigging fools?   136
Companion, hence!

CASSIUS   Away, away, begone!   *Exit Poet.* 137

BRUTUS
Lucilius and Titinius, bid the commanders
Prepare to lodge their companies tonight.

CASSIUS
And come yourselves, and bring Messala with you
Immediately to us.   [*Exeunt Lucilius and Titinius.*]

BRUTUS [*To Lucius within*]   Lucius, a bowl of wine.

CASSIUS
I did not think you could have been so angry.

BRUTUS
O Cassius, I am sick of many griefs.

CASSIUS
Of your philosophy you make no use
If you give place to accidental evils.   145

BRUTUS
No man bears sorrow better. Portia is dead.

CASSIUS   Ha? Portia?

BRUTUS   She is dead.

CASSIUS
How scaped I killing when I crossed you so?   149
O insupportable and touching loss!   150
Upon what sickness?

BRUTUS   Impatient of my absence,   151
And grief that young Octavius with Mark Antony
Have made themselves so strong—for with her death   153
That tidings came—with this she fell distract
And, her attendants absent, swallowed fire.   155

CASSIUS
And died so?

BRUTUS   Even so.

CASSIUS   O ye immortal gods!

136 jigging rhyming in jerky doggerel   137 Companion fellow
145 accidental evils misfortunes caused by chance (which should be a
matter of indifference to a philosopher like Brutus)   149 scaped I
killing did I escape being killed   150 touching grievous   151 Impatient
of unable to endure   153 her death i.e., news of her death
155 swallowed fire (According to Plutarch, as translated by Thomas
North, Portia "took hot burning coals and cast them in her mouth, and
kept her mouth so close that she choked herself.")

Enter Boy [Lucius] with wine and tapers.

BRUTUS
　Speak no more of her.—Give me a bowl of wine.—
　In this I bury all unkindness, Cassius.   *Drinks.*
CASSIUS
　My heart is thirsty for that noble pledge.
　Fill, Lucius, till the wine o'erswell the cup;
　I cannot drink too much of Brutus' love.   161
                          [*He drinks. Exit Lucius.*]

　　Enter Titinius and Messala.

BRUTUS
　Come in, Titinius. Welcome, good Messala.
　Now sit we close about this taper here
　And call in question our necessities.   [*They sit.*] 164
CASSIUS
　Portia, art thou gone?
BRUTUS   No more, I pray you.
　Messala, I have here receivèd letters
　That young Octavius and Mark Antony
　Come down upon us with a mighty power,   168
　Bending their expedition toward Philippi.   169
                          [*He shows letters.*]

MESSALA
　Myself have letters of the selfsame tenor.
BRUTUS   With what addition?
MESSALA
　That by proscription and bills of outlawry   172
　Octavius, Antony, and Lepidus
　Have put to death an hundred senators.
BRUTUS
　Therein our letters do not well agree;
　Mine speak of seventy senators that died
　By their proscriptions, Cicero being one.
CASSIUS
　Cicero one?

161 s.d. Titinius (Lucilius does not return with Titinius, as he was
ordered to do at ll. 140–141, probably because he was not in Shakespeare's original version of this scene.)   **164 call in question** examine,
discuss   **168 power** army   **169 Bending** directing.   **expedition** rapid
march; military power   **172 proscription** (See 4.1.17, note.)

MESSALA   Cicero is dead,
And by that order of proscription.
Had you your letters from your wife, my lord?   180
BRUTUS   No, Messala.
MESSALA
Nor nothing in your letters writ of her?   182
BRUTUS
Nothing, Messala.
MESSALA   That, methinks, is strange.
BRUTUS
Why ask you? Hear you aught of her in yours?
MESSALA   No, my lord.
BRUTUS
Now, as you are a Roman, tell me true.
MESSALA
Then like a Roman bear the truth I tell,
For certain she is dead, and by strange manner.
BRUTUS
Why, farewell, Portia. We must die, Messala.
With meditating that she must die once,   190
I have the patience to endure it now.
MESSALA
Even so great men great losses should endure.   192
CASSIUS
I have as much of this in art as you,   193
But yet my nature could not bear it so.   194
BRUTUS
Well, to our work alive. What do you think   195
Of marching to Philippi presently?
CASSIUS
I do not think it good.
BRUTUS   Your reason?
CASSIUS   This it is:

180–194 Had . . . so (This passage is sometimes regarded as contradic-
tory to and redundant of ll. 142–165. Perhaps it is the original account
of Portia's death, and ll. 142–165 are part of a later interpolation, but it
is also possible that both are intended, the first being Brutus' intimate
revelation of the news to his friend and the second, Brutus' recovery of
his stoic reserve now on display for Messala and Titinius.)   182 nothing
. . . her nothing written about her in the letters you've received
190 once at some time   192 Even so in just such a way   193 art i.e., the
acquired wisdom of stoical fortitude   195 alive concerning us who are
alive and dealing with present realities

'Tis better that the enemy seek us.
So shall he waste his means, weary his soldiers,
Doing himself offense, whilst we, lying still,   200
Are full of rest, defense, and nimbleness.

BRUTUS
Good reasons must of force give place to better.   202
The people twixt Philippi and this ground
Do stand but in a forced affection,
For they have grudged us contribution.
The enemy, marching along by them,
By them shall make a fuller number up,
Come on refreshed, new-added, and encouraged;   208
From which advantage shall we cut him off
If at Philippi we do face him there,
These people at our back.

CASSIUS   Hear me, good brother—

BRUTUS
Under your pardon. You must note besides   212
That we have tried the utmost of our friends;
Our legions are brim full, our cause is ripe.
The enemy increaseth every day;
We, at the height, are ready to decline.
There is a tide in the affairs of men
Which, taken at the flood, leads on to fortune;
Omitted, all the voyage of their life   219
Is bound in shallows and in miseries.   220
On such a full sea are we now afloat,
And we must take the current when it serves
Or lose our ventures.

CASSIUS   Then, with your will, go on.   223
We'll along ourselves and meet them at Philippi.   224

BRUTUS
The deep of night is crept upon our talk,
And nature must obey necessity,
Which we will niggard with a little rest.   227
There is no more to say?

200 offense harm   **202 of force** necessarily   **208 new-added** reinforced   **212 Under your pardon** i.e., excuse me, let me continue
219 Omitted neglected, missed   **220 bound in** confined to
223 ventures investments (of enterprise at sea).   **with your will** as you
wish   **224 along** go along   **227 niggard** stint (by sleeping only briefly)

CASSIUS   No more. Good night.
Early tomorrow will we rise and hence.   229
BRUTUS
Lucius! (*Enter Lucius.*) My gown. [*Exit Lucius.*] Fare-
well, good Messala.   230
Good night, Titinius. Noble, noble Cassius,
Good night and good repose.
CASSIUS   O my dear brother!
This was an ill beginning of the night.
Never come such division 'tween our souls!
Let it not, Brutus.

    Enter Lucius with the gown.

BRUTUS   Everything is well.
CASSIUS   Good night, my lord.
BRUTUS   Good night, good brother.
TITINIUS, MESSALA   Good night, Lord Brutus.
BRUTUS   Farewell, everyone.
                    Exeunt [all but Brutus and Lucius].
Give me the gown. Where is thy instrument?   241
LUCIUS
Here in the tent.
BRUTUS   What, thou speak'st drowsily?
Poor knave, I blame thee not; thou art o'erwatched.   243
Call Claudius and some other of my men;
I'll have them sleep on cushions in my tent.
LUCIUS   Varro and Claudius!

    Enter Varro and Claudius.

VARRO   Calls my lord?
BRUTUS
I pray you, sirs, lie in my tent and sleep.
It may be I shall raise you by and by   249
On business to my brother Cassius.
VARRO
So please you, we will stand and watch your pleasure. 251
BRUTUS
I will not have it so. Lie down, good sirs.

---

229 hence depart   **230 gown** dressing gown   **241 instrument** i.e., lute or
cithern   **243 knave** boy.   **o'erwatched** tired from lack of sleep   **249 raise**
rouse   **251 watch your pleasure** wakefully await your commands

It may be I shall otherwise bethink me.   253

                [*Varro and Claudius lie down.*]

Look, Lucius, here's the book I sought for so;

I put it in the pocket of my gown.

LUCIUS

I was sure your lordship did not give it me.

BRUTUS

Bear with me, good boy, I am much forgetful.

Canst thou hold up thy heavy eyes awhile

And touch thy instrument a strain or two?   259

LUCIUS

Ay, my lord, an 't please you.

BRUTUS   It does, my boy.   260

I trouble thee too much, but thou art willing.

LUCIUS   It is my duty, sir.

BRUTUS

I should not urge thy duty past thy might;

I know young bloods look for a time of rest.   264

LUCIUS   I have slept, my lord, already.

BRUTUS

It was well done, and thou shalt sleep again;

I will not hold thee long. If I do live,

I will be good to thee.

             Music, and a song. [*Lucius falls asleep.*]

This is a sleepy tune. O murderous slumber,   269

Layest thou thy leaden mace upon my boy,   270

That plays thee music? Gentle knave, good night;

I will not do thee so much wrong to wake thee.

If thou dost nod, thou break'st thy instrument;

I'll take it from thee. And, good boy, good night.

              [*He removes Lucius' instrument,*

                    and begins to read.]

Let me see, let me see; is not the leaf turned down

Where I left reading? Here it is, I think.

    Enter the Ghost of Caesar.

---

253 otherwise bethink me change my mind   **259 touch** i.e., play on.
strain tune, musical phrase   **260 an 't** if it   **264 young bloods** youthful
constitutions   **269 murderous** producing the likeness of death
270 leaden mace heavy staff of office (used by a sheriff to touch the
shoulder of one being placed under arrest)

How ill this taper burns! Ha! Who comes here?   277
I think it is the weakness of mine eyes
That shapes this monstrous apparition.
It comes upon me.—Art thou any thing?   280
Art thou some god, some angel, or some devil,
That mak'st my blood cold and my hair to stare?   282
Speak to me what thou art.
GHOST
Thy evil spirit, Brutus.
BRUTUS   Why com'st thou?
GHOST
To tell thee thou shalt see me at Philippi.
BRUTUS   Well; then I shall see thee again?
GHOST   Ay, at Philippi.
BRUTUS
Why, I will see thee at Philippi, then.   [*Exit Ghost.*]
Now I have taken heart, thou vanishest.
Ill spirit, I would hold more talk with thee.—
Boy, Lucius! Varro! Claudius! Sirs, awake!
Claudius!
LUCIUS   The strings, my lord, are false.   292
BRUTUS
He thinks he still is at his instrument.
Lucius, awake!
LUCIUS   My lord?
BRUTUS
Didst thou dream, Lucius, that thou so criedst out?
LUCIUS
My lord, I do not know that I did cry.
BRUTUS
Yes, that thou didst. Didst thou see anything?
LUCIUS   Nothing, my lord.
BRUTUS
Sleep again, Lucius. Sirrah Claudius!
[*To Varro.*] Fellow thou, awake!
VARRO   My lord?
CLAUDIUS   My lord?

277 How . . . burns (It is part of the machinery of apparitions that lights
burn low and blue.)   **280 upon** toward   **282 stare** stand on end
292 false out of tune

[They get up.]

BRUTUS
  Why did you so cry out, sirs, in your sleep?
VARRO, CLAUDIUS
  Did we, my lord?
BRUTUS   Ay. Saw you anything?
VARRO
  No, my lord, I saw nothing.
CLAUDIUS   Nor I, my lord.
BRUTUS
  Go and commend me to my brother Cassius.   305
  Bid him set on his powers betimes before,   306
  And we will follow.
VARRO, CLAUDIUS   It shall be done, my lord.
                                          Exeunt.

✤

---

305 commend me deliver my greetings **306 set . . . before** advance his
troops early in the morning, before me

5.1   *Enter Octavius, Antony, and their army.*

OCTAVIUS
  Now, Antony, our hopes are answerèd.
  You said the enemy would not come down,
  But keep the hills and upper regions.   3
  It proves not so. Their battles are at hand;   4
  They mean to warn us at Philippi here,   5
  Answering before we do demand of them.
ANTONY
  Tut, I am in their bosoms, and I know   7
  Wherefore they do it. They could be content
  To visit other places, and come down   9
  With fearful bravery, thinking by this face   10
  To fasten in our thoughts that they have courage;   11
  But 'tis not so.

        Enter a Messenger.

MESSENGER   Prepare you, generals.   12
  The enemy comes on in gallant show.
  Their bloody sign of battle is hung out,   14
  And something to be done immediately.   15
ANTONY
  Octavius, lead your battle softly on   16
  Upon the left hand of the even field.
OCTAVIUS
  Upon the right hand, I. Keep thou the left.
ANTONY
  Why do you cross me in this exigent?   19
OCTAVIUS
  I do not cross you, but I will do so.   *March.*   20

        Drum. Enter Brutus, Cassius, and their army;
        [Lucilius, Titinius, Messala, and others].

5.1. Location: The plains of Philippi, in Macedonia.
3 keep remain in **4 battles** armies **5 warn** challenge **7 bosoms** secret
councils **9 visit other places** i.e., be elsewhere. **come** they come
10 fearful bravery (1) awesome ostentation (2) a show of bravery to
conceal their fear. **face** pretense (of courage) **11 fasten** fix the idea
12 'tis not so (1) their plan cannot deceive us (2) they have no courage
14 bloody sign red flag **15 to be** is to be **16 softly** warily, with re-
straint **19 cross** contradict. **exigent** critical moment **20 do so** i.e., do
as I said

BRUTUS   They stand and would have parley.
CASSIUS
  Stand fast, Titinius. We must out and talk.   22
OCTAVIUS
  Mark Antony, shall we give sign of battle?
ANTONY
  No, Caesar, we will answer on their charge.   24
  Make forth. The generals would have some words.   25
OCTAVIUS *[To his officers]*   Stir not until the signal.
         [The two sides advance toward one another.]
BRUTUS
  Words before blows. Is it so, countrymen?
OCTAVIUS
  Not that we love words better, as you do.
BRUTUS
  Good words are better than bad strokes, Octavius.
ANTONY
  In your bad strokes, Brutus, you give good words.   30
  Witness the hole you made in Caesar's heart,
  Crying, "Long live! Hail, Caesar!"
CASSIUS   Antony,
  The posture of your blows are yet unknown;   33
  But for your words, they rob the Hybla bees,   34
  And leave them honeyless.
ANTONY   Not stingless too?
BRUTUS   O, yes, and soundless too.
  For you have stolen their buzzing, Antony,
  And very wisely threat before you sting.   39
ANTONY
  Villains! You did not so when your vile daggers   40
  Hacked one another in the sides of Caesar.
  You showed your teeth like apes, and fawned like
    hounds,   42

22 out go out   **24 answer on their charge** respond when they attack
25 Make forth march forward   **30 In . . . words** i.e., as you deliver cruel
blows, Brutus, you use deceiving flattery. (Antony deliberately changes
Brutus' *Good words* in l. 29, "bravely spoken words," into a negative
meaning.)   **33 posture** quality   **34 for** as for.   **Hybla** a mountain and a
town in ancient Sicily, famous for honey   **39 very wisely** (Said ironi-
cally; Brutus suggests that Antony is all bluster and no action.)   **threat**
threaten   **40 so** i.e., give warning   **42 showed your teeth** i.e., in smiles

And bowed like bondmen, kissing Caesar's feet,
Whilst damnèd Casca, like a cur, behind
Struck Caesar on the neck. O you flatterers!

CASSIUS
Flatterers? Now, Brutus, thank yourself!
This tongue had not offended so today
If Cassius might have ruled.   48

OCTAVIUS
Come, come, the cause. If arguing make us sweat,   49
The proof of it will turn to redder drops.   50
Look,   [*He draws*]
I draw a sword against conspirators.
When think you that the sword goes up again?   53
Never, till Caesar's three-and-thirty wounds   54
Be well avenged, or till another Caesar
Have added slaughter to the sword of traitors.   56

BRUTUS
Caesar, thou canst not die by traitors' hands,   57
Unless thou bring'st them with thee.

OCTAVIUS   So I hope.   58
I was not born to die on Brutus' sword.   59

BRUTUS
O, if thou wert the noblest of thy strain,   60
Young man, thou couldst not die more honorable.

CASSIUS
A peevish schoolboy, worthless of such honor,   62
Joined with a masker and a reveler!   63

ANTONY
Old Cassius still.

OCTAVIUS   Come, Antony, away!—
Defiance, traitors, hurl we in your teeth.

48 ruled prevailed (in urging that Antony be killed) **49 the cause** to our
business **50 proof** trial **53 up** in its sheath **54 three-and-thirty**
(Plutarch has it three-and-twenty.) **56 Have . . . to** has also been slaugh-
tered by **57–59 Caesar . . . sword** (Brutus says that if there are any
traitors on the battlefield they will perforce be in Octavius' army;
Octavius twists Brutus' taunt by pretending that Brutus meant Octavius
could not die on Brutus' sword.) **60 if** even if. **strain** lineage
62 peevish silly, childish. **schoolboy** (Octavius was 18 at the time of
Caesar's assassination.) **worthless** unworthy **63 masker . . . reveler**
i.e., Antony, noted for his reveling

If you dare fight today, come to the field;
If not, when you have stomachs.   67
                    Exeunt Octavius, Antony, and army.

CASSIUS
Why now, blow wind, swell billow, and swim bark!   68
The storm is up, and all is on the hazard.   69

BRUTUS
Lo, Lucilius! Hark, a word with you.

LUCILIUS (*Stands forth*)   My lord?
                    [*Brutus and Lucilius converse apart.*]

CASSIUS   Messala!

MESSALA (*Stands forth*)   What says my general?

CASSIUS   Messala,
This is my birthday; as this very day   75
Was Cassius born. Give me thy hand, Messala.
Be thou my witness that against my will,
As Pompey was, am I compelled to set   78
Upon one battle all our liberties.
You know that I held Epicurus strong   80
And his opinion. Now I change my mind
And partly credit things that do presage.   82
Coming from Sardis, on our former ensign   83
Two mighty eagles fell, and there they perched,   84
Gorging and feeding from our soldiers' hands,
Who to Philippi here consorted us.   86
This morning are they fled away and gone,
And in their steads do ravens, crows, and kites   88
Fly o'er our heads and downward look on us
As we were sickly prey. Their shadows seem   90
A canopy most fatal, under which   91
Our army lies, ready to give up the ghost.

MESSALA
Believe not so.

67 stomachs (1) appetites (for fighting) (2) courage   **68 billow** wave
69 on the hazard at stake   **75 as** on   **78 Pompey** (The reference is to the
battle of Pharsalus, where Pompey was persuaded to fight Caesar
against his own judgment.)   **set** stake   **80 Epicurus** Greek philosopher
(341–270 B.C.), whose materialistic philosophy spurned belief in omens
or superstitions   **82 presage** foretell events   **83 former ensign** foremost
standard, the legion's *aquila*, a tall standard surmounted by the image
of an eagle   **84 fell** swooped down   **86 consorted** accompanied
88 kites birds of prey, belonging to the hawk family   **90 As** as if
91 fatāl presaging death

CASSIUS   I but believe it partly,   93
    For I am fresh of spirit and resolved
    To meet all perils very constantly.   95
BRUTUS
    Even so, Lucilius.   *[He rejoins Cassius.]*
CASSIUS   Now, most noble Brutus,   96
    The gods today stand friendly, that we may,   97
    Lovers in peace, lead on our days to age!   98
    But since the affairs of men rest still incertain,   99
    Let's reason with the worst that may befall.   100
    If we do lose this battle, then is this
    The very last time we shall speak together.
    What are you then determinèd to do?
BRUTUS
    Even by the rule of that philosophy
    By which I did blame Cato for the death   105
    Which he did give himself—I know not how,
    But I do find it cowardly and vile,
    For fear of what might fall, so to prevent   108
    The time of life—arming myself with patience   109
    To stay the providence of some high powers   110
    That govern us below.
CASSIUS   Then, if we lose this battle,
    You are contented to be led in triumph
    Thorough the streets of Rome?   113
BRUTUS
    No, Cassius, no. Think not, thou noble Roman,
    That ever Brutus will go bound to Rome;
    He bears too great a mind. But this same day
    Must end that work the ides of March begun.
    And whether we shall meet again I know not;
    Therefore our everlasting farewell take.
    Forever and forever farewell, Cassius!
    If we do meet again, why, we shall smile;
    If not, why then this parting was well made.

---

93 but only   **95 constantly** resolutely   **96 Even so, Lucilius** (This phrase marks the end of Brutus' private conversation apart with Lucilius.) **97 The gods** may the gods   **98 Lovers** friends   **99 still** always **100 reason** reckon   **105 Cato** i.e., Marcus Porcius Cato, Brutus' father-in-law, who killed himself to avoid submission to Caesar in 46 B.C. (See 2.1.296 and note.)   **108 fall** befall.   **prevent** anticipate the end, cut short   **109 time** term, end   **110 stay** await   **113 Thorough** through

CASSIUS
    Forever and forever farewell, Brutus!
    If we do meet again, we'll smile indeed;
    If not, 'tis true this parting was well made.
BRUTUS
    Why then, lead on. O, that a man might know
    The end of this day's business ere it come!
    But it sufficeth that the day will end,
    And then the end is known. Come, ho, away!

                                              Exeunt.

5.2   *Alarum. Enter Brutus and Messala.*

BRUTUS
    Ride, ride, Messala, ride, and give these bills   1
    Unto the legions on the other side.   2
                        [*He hands him written orders.*]
                                        Loud alarum.
    Let them set on at once; for I perceive   3
    But cold demeanor in Octavius' wing,   4
    And sudden push gives them the overthrow.
    Ride, ride, Messala! Let them all come down.   6
                                              Exeunt.

5.3   *Alarums. Enter Cassius [carrying a standard],
           and Titinius.*

CASSIUS
    O, look, Titinius, look, the villains fly!   1
    Myself have to mine own turned enemy.   2
    This ensign here of mine was turning back;   3

5.2. Location: The plains of Philippi. The field of battle.
s.d. Alarum (This is seemingly an anticipatory stage direction; the battle
actually begins with the *Loud alarum* at l. 2. An *alarum* is offstage
sounds signifying a battle.) **1 bills** orders **2 side** wing (i.e., Cassius'
wing) **3 set on** attack **4 cold demeanor** faintheartedness **6 come
down** i.e., from the hills where they have been awaiting the battle; see
5.1.2–3.

5.3. Location: The field of battle still.
1 the villains i.e., my own troops **2 mine own** my own men
3 ensign bearer of the standard. (A legion's *aquila* or eagle standard had
great moral significance and needed to be guarded.)

I slew the coward and did take it from him.   4
TITINIUS
O Cassius, Brutus gave the word too early,
Who, having some advantage on Octavius,
Took it too eagerly. His soldiers fell to spoil,   7
Whilst we by Antony are all enclosed.   8

Enter Pindarus.

PINDARUS
Fly further off, my lord, fly further off!
Mark Antony is in your tents, my lord.
Fly therefore, noble Cassius, fly far off.
CASSIUS
This hill is far enough. Look, look, Titinius:
Are those my tents where I perceive the fire?
TITINIUS
They are, my lord.
CASSIUS   Titinius, if thou lovest me,
Mount thou my horse and hide thy spurs in him
Till he have brought thee up to yonder troops
And here again, that I may rest assured
Whether yond troops are friend or enemy.
TITINIUS
I will be here again even with a thought.   *Exit.* 19
CASSIUS
Go, Pindarus, get higher on that hill.
My sight was ever thick. Regard Titinius,   21
And tell me what thou not'st about the field.   22
                [*Pindarus goes up.*]
This day I breathèd first. Time is come round,   23
And where I did begin, there shall I end.
My life is run his compass.—Sirrah, what news?   25
PINDARUS (*Above*) O my lord!
CASSIUS What news?

4 it i.e., the ensign's standard **7 spoil** looting **8 enclosed** surrounded
19 even . . . thought as quick as thought **21 thick** imperfect, dim. **Regard** observe **22 s.d. Pindarus goes up** (Pindarus may exit and ascend
behind the scenes to the gallery; at l. 35 he does *enter* in order to return.) **23 breathèd first** i.e., is my birthday **25 his compass** its circuit,
circle (as drawn by a geometer's compass)

PINDARUS [*Above*]
Titinius is enclosèd round about
With horsemen that make to him on the spur,   29
Yet he spurs on. Now they are almost on him.
Now, Titinius! Now some light. O, he   31
Lights too. He's ta'en. (*Shout.*) And hark! They shout for
   joy.
CASSIUS   Come down, behold no more.
O coward that I am, to live so long
To see my best friend ta'en before my face!

   Enter Pindarus [*from above*].

Come hither, sirrah.
In Parthia did I take thee prisoner,   37
And then I swore thee, saving of thy life,   38
That whatsoever I did bid thee do
Thou shouldst attempt it. Come now, keep thine oath;
Now be a freeman, and with this good sword,
That ran through Caesar's bowels, search this bosom.   42
Stand not to answer. Here, take thou the hilts,   43
And when my face is covered, as 'tis now,
Guide thou the sword. [*Pindarus does so.*] Caesar, thou
   art revenged,
Even with the sword that killed thee.   [*He dies.*]
PINDARUS
So, I am free, yet would not so have been   47
Durst I have done my will. O Cassius!   48
Far from this country Pindarus shall run,
Where never Roman shall take note of him.   [*Exit.*]

   Enter Titinius [*with a garland of laurel*] *and
   Messala.*

MESSALA
It is but change, Titinius; for Octavius   51
Is overthrown by noble Brutus' power,

29 make . . . spur approach him riding rapidly   **31 light** alight, dis-
mount   **37 Parthia** (What is now northern Iran.)   **38 swore . . . of** made
you swear, when I spared   **42 search** penetrate   **43 Stand** delay.   **hilts**
i.e., sword hilt   **47 so** in this manner   **48 Durst** dared   **51 change**
exchange of advantage, quid pro quo

As Cassius' legions are by Antony.

TITINIUS
These tidings will well comfort Cassius.

MESSALA
Where did you leave him?

TITINIUS   All disconsolate,
With Pindarus his bondman, on this hill.

MESSALA
Is not that he that lies upon the ground?

TITINIUS
He lies not like the living. O my heart!

MESSALA
Is not that he?

TITINIUS   No, this was he, Messala,
But Cassius is no more. O setting sun,
As in thy red rays thou dost sink to night,   61
So in his red blood Cassius' day is set!
The sun of Rome is set. Our day is gone;   63
Clouds, dews, and dangers come; our deeds are done!
Mistrust of my success hath done this deed.   65

MESSALA
Mistrust of good success hath done this deed.
O hateful Error, Melancholy's child,   67
Why dost thou show to the apt thoughts of men   68
The things that are not? O Error, soon conceived,
Thou never com'st unto a happy birth,
But kill'st the mother that engendered thee.   71

TITINIUS
What, Pindarus! Where art thou, Pindarus?

MESSALA
Seek him, Titinius, whilst I go to meet
The noble Brutus, thrusting this report
Into his ears. I may say "thrusting" it;
For piercing steel and darts envenomèd   76
Shall be as welcome to the ears of Brutus
As tidings of this sight.

---

61 to toward **63 sun** (with pun on *son*) **65 Mistrust** i.e., Cassius'
doubt **67 Melancholy's child** i.e., chimera bred of a melancholic temperament **68 apt** impressionable **71 the mother** i.e., the melancholy
person who too readily believed the worst **76 darts** spears

TITINIUS   Hie you, Messala,   78
  And I will seek for Pindarus the while.
                                        [*Exit Messala.*]
  Why didst thou send me forth, brave Cassius?
  Did I not meet thy friends? And did not they
  Put on my brows this wreath of victory
  And bid me give it thee? Didst thou not hear their
    shouts?
  Alas, thou hast misconstrued everything.
  But, hold thee, take this garland on thy brow.   85
      [*He places a garland on Cassius' brow.*]
  Thy Brutus bid me give it thee, and I
  Will do his bidding. Brutus, come apace   87
  And see how I regarded Caius Cassius.
  By your leave, gods! This is a Roman's part.
  Come, Cassius' sword, and find Titinius' heart.
                          [*He stabs himself and*] *dies.*

    Alarum. Enter Brutus, Messala, young Cato,
    Strato, Volumnius, and Lucilius, [*Labeo, and*
    Flavius].

BRUTUS
  Where, where, Messala, doth his body lie?
MESSALA
  Lo, yonder, and Titinius mourning it.
BRUTUS
  Titinius' face is upward.
CATO   He is slain.
BRUTUS
  O Julius Caesar, thou art mighty yet!
  Thy spirit walks abroad and turns our swords
  In our own proper entrails.   *Low alarums.*
CATO   Brave Titinius!   96
  Look whe'er he have not crowned dead Cassius.   97
BRUTUS
  Are yet two Romans living such as these?
  The last of all the Romans, fare thee well!
  It is impossible that ever Rome
  Should breed thy fellow. Friends, I owe more tears

78 Hie hasten **85 hold thee** wait **87 apace** quickly **96 own proper**
very own **97 whe'er** whether

To this dead man than you shall see me pay.—
I shall find time, Cassius, I shall find time.—
Come, therefore, and to Thasos send his body.   104
His funerals shall not be in our camp,
Lest it discomfort us. Lucilius, come,   106
And come, young Cato, let us to the field.
Labeo and Flavius, set our battles on.   108
'Tis three o'clock, and, Romans, yet ere night
We shall try fortune in a second fight.   *Exeunt.* 110

5.4   *Alarum. Enter Brutus, Messala, [young] Cato,
Lucilius, and Flavius.*

BRUTUS
Yet, countrymen, O, yet hold up your heads!
            [*Exit, followed by Messala and Flavius.*]
CATO
What bastard doth not? Who will go with me?   2
I will proclaim my name about the field:
I am the son of Marcus Cato, ho!
A foe to tyrants, and my country's friend.
I am the son of Marcus Cato, ho!

        Enter soldiers, and fight.

LUCILIUS
And I am Brutus, Marcus Brutus I!
Brutus, my country's friend! Know me for Brutus!
            [*Young Cato is slain by Antony's men.*]
O young and noble Cato, art thou down?
Why, now thou diest as bravely as Titinius,
And mayst be honored, being Cato's son.
FIRST SOLDIER [*Capturing Lucilius*]
Yield, or thou diest.
LUCILIUS [*Offering money*]   Only I yield to die.   12

---

104 Thasos an island off the coast of Thrace, near Philippi
106 discomfort discourage   **108 battles** armies   **110 s.d. Exeunt** (The
bodies of Cassius and Titinius are probably carried off at this point.)

5.4. Location: Scene continues at the field of battle.
2 What . . . not who is so base that he would not do so   **12 Only . . . die**
i.e., I surrender only to die immediately

There is so much that thou wilt kill me straight;   13
Kill Brutus, and be honored in his death.

FIRST SOLDIER
We must not. A noble prisoner!

SECOND SOLDIER
Room, ho! Tell Antony, Brutus is ta'en.

    Enter Antony.

FIRST SOLDIER
I'll tell the news. Here comes the General.—
Brutus is ta'en, Brutus is ta'en, my lord.

ANTONY   Where is he?

LUCILIUS
Safe, Antony, Brutus is safe enough.
I dare assure thee that no enemy
Shall ever take alive the noble Brutus.
The gods defend him from so great a shame!
When you do find him, or alive or dead,   24
He will be found like Brutus, like himself.

ANTONY [*To First Soldier*]
This is not Brutus, friend, but, I assure you,
A prize no less in worth. Keep this man safe;
Give him all kindness. I had rather have
Such men my friends than enemies. Go on,
And see whe'er Brutus be alive or dead;   30
And bring us word unto Octavius' tent
How everything is chanced.   *Exeunt* [*separately*]. 32

5.5   *Enter Brutus, Dardanius, Clitus, Strato, and
Volumnius.*

BRUTUS
Come, poor remains of friends, rest on this rock.
                           [*He sits.*]

---

13 There . . . straight i.e., here is money (or perhaps the inducement of
honor) if you will kill me at once   **24 or alive** either alive   **30 whe'er**
whether   **32 is chanced** has fallen out   **s.d. Exeunt** (The body of
young Cato may be carried off at this point; it is not seen by Brutus et
al. in scene 5.)

5.5. Location: The field of battle still.

CLITUS
  Statilius showed the torchlight, but, my lord,   2
  He came not back. He is or ta'en or slain.   3
BRUTUS
  Sit thee down, Clitus. Slaying is the word.
  It is a deed in fashion. Hark thee, Clitus.
                              [*He whispers.*]
CLITUS
  What, I, my lord? No, not for all the world.
BRUTUS
  Peace then. No words.
CLITUS   I'll rather kill myself.
BRUTUS
  Hark thee, Dardanius.   [*He whispers.*]
DARDANIUS   Shall I do such a deed?
        [*Dardanius and Clitus move away from Brutus.*]
CLITUS   O Dardanius!
DARDANIUS   O Clitus!
CLITUS
  What ill request did Brutus make to thee?
DARDANIUS
  To kill him, Clitus. Look, he meditates.
CLITUS
  Now is that noble vessel full of grief,
  That it runs over even at his eyes.
BRUTUS
  Come hither, good Volumnius. List a word.   15
VOLUMNIUS
  What says my lord?
BRUTUS   Why, this, Volumnius:
  The ghost of Caesar hath appeared to me
  Two several times by night—at Sardis once,   18
  And this last night here in Philippi fields.
  I know my hour is come.
VOLUMNIUS   Not so, my lord.
BRUTUS
  Nay, I am sure it is, Volumnius.
  Thou seest the world, Volumnius, how it goes;

2 Statilius . . . torchlight (A scout named Statilius has gone to see if
Cassius' camp is still occupied; he signals back, but is taken or
slain.) **3 or ta'en** either taken **15 List** listen to **18 several** separate

Our enemies have beat us to the pit.   *Low alarums.* 23
It is more worthy to leap in ourselves
Than tarry till they push us. Good Volumnius,
Thou know'st that we two went to school together.
Even for that, our love of old, I prithee,   27
Hold thou my sword hilts whilst I run on it.   28

VOLUMNIUS
That's not an office for a friend, my lord.   29
                                        Alarum still.

CLITUS
Fly, fly, my lord! There is no tarrying here.

BRUTUS
Farewell to you, and you, and you, Volumnius.
Strato, thou hast been all this while asleep;
Farewell to thee too, Strato. Countrymen,
My heart doth joy that yet in all my life
I found no man but he was true to me.
I shall have glory by this losing day
More than Octavius and Mark Antony
By this vile conquest shall attain unto.   38
So fare you well at once, for Brutus' tongue   39
Hath almost ended his life's history.
Night hangs upon mine eyes; my bones would rest,
That have but labored to attain this hour.   42
                Alarum. Cry within, "Fly, fly, fly!"

CLITUS
Fly, my lord, fly!

BRUTUS   Hence, I will follow.
            [*Exeunt Clitus, Dardanius, and Volumnius.*]
I prithee, Strato, stay thou by thy lord.
Thou art a fellow of a good respect;   45
Thy life hath had some smatch of honor in it.   46
Hold then my sword, and turn away thy face,
While I do run upon it. Wilt thou, Strato?

STRATO
Give me your hand first. Fare you well, my lord.

---

23 beat driven. **pit** trap for wild animals; also, a grave   **27 that, our love** that friendship of ours   **28 hilts** i.e., hilt   **29 office** duty   **38 vile** paltry   **39 at once** all together   **42 That . . . hour** i.e., all their striving has been toward this moment of death   **45 respect** reputation   **46 some smatch** some flavor, a touch

BRUTUS
Farewell, good Strato. [*He runs on his sword.*] Caesar,
now be still.
I killed not thee with half so good a will.   *Dies.* 51

*Alarum. Retreat. Enter Antony, Octavius; Messala,
Lucilius [as prisoners]; and the army.*

OCTAVIUS   What man is that?
MESSALA
My master's man. Strato, where is thy master?
STRATO
Free from the bondage you are in, Messala.
The conquerors can but make a fire of him,
For Brutus only overcame himself,   56
And no man else hath honor by his death.
LUCILIUS
So Brutus should be found. I thank thee, Brutus,
That thou hast proved Lucilius' saying true.   59
OCTAVIUS
All that served Brutus, I will entertain them.   60
Fellow, wilt thou bestow thy time with me?
STRATO
Ay, if Messala will prefer me to you.   62
OCTAVIUS   Do so, good Messala.
MESSALA   How died my master, Strato?
STRATO
I held the sword, and he did run on it.
MESSALA
Octavius, then take him to follow thee,   66
That did the latest service to my master.   67
ANTONY
This was the noblest Roman of them all.
All the conspirators save only he
Did that they did in envy of great Caesar;   70
He only in a general honest thought
And common good to all made one of them.

51 s.d. Retreat signal to retire   **56 Brutus . . . himself** only Brutus
conquered Brutus   **59 saying** (See 5.4.21–25.)   **60 entertain** take into
service   **62 prefer** recommend   **66 follow** serve   **67 latest** last   **70 that**
what.   **envy of** malice toward

His life was gentle, and the elements   73
So mixed in him that Nature might stand up
And say to all the world, "This was a man!"

OCTAVIUS
According to his virtue let us use him,
With all respect and rites of burial.
Within my tent his bones tonight shall lie,
Most like a soldier, ordered honorably.   79
So call the field to rest, and let's away   80
To part the glories of this happy day.   81

        Exeunt omnes [*with Brutus' body*].

---

73 gentle noble.   **elements** (Man as a microcosm is made up of earth,
air, fire, and water, whose qualities were mingled in Brutus in due
proportions.)   **79 ordered** treated, arranged for   **80 field** army in the
field   **81 part** share   **s.d. omnes** all

Date and Text

Julius Caesar was first published in the First Folio of 1623.
The text is an excellent one, based evidently on a theater
promptbook or a transcript of it. In the Folio the play is
included among the tragedies and entitled *The Tragedy of
Julius Caesar,* although the table of contents lists it as *The
Life and death of Julius Caesar.*

First performance must have occurred in 1599 or slightly
earlier. On September 21, 1599, a Swiss visitor named
Thomas Platter crossed the Thames River after lunch with
a company of spectators to see "the tragedy of the first Emperor Julius Caesar" performed in a thatched-roofed building. The description fits the Globe, the Rose, and the Swan
theaters, but the last of these was not in regular use. The
Admiral's men at the Rose are not known to have had a
Caesar play, whereas the Chamberlain's men certainly had
Shakespeare's play about this time. They had only recently
moved from their Theatre in the northeast suburbs of Lon
don to the Globe south of the river, and *Julius Caesar* and
Henry V were probably new plays for the occasion.

John Weever, in *The Mirror of Martyrs* (1601), is surely re-
ferring to Shakespeare's play when he describes "the
many-headed multitude" listening first to "Brutus' speech
that Caesar was ambitious" and then to "eloquent Mark
Antony." (The dedication to Weever's book claims he wrote
it "some two years ago," in 1599; but since this book has
been shown to be heavily indebted to a work that first appeared in 1600, Weever's allusion is not as helpful in limit-
ing the date as was once thought.) Ben Jonson's *Every Man
in His Humor,* acted in 1599, may also contain allusions to
Shakespeare's play.

Textual Notes

These textual notes are not a historical collation, either of the early folios or of more recent editions; they are simply a record of departures in this edition from the copy text. The reading adopted in this edition appears in bold face, followed by the rejected reading from the copy text, i.e., the First Folio. Only major alterations in punctuation are noted. Changes in lineation are not indicated, nor are some minor and obvious typographical errors.

Abbreviations used:
F the First Folio
s.d. stage direction
s.p. speech prefix

Copy text: the First Folio.

1.1. s.d. [and elsewhere] Marullus Murellus **37 Pompey . . . oft** Pompey many a time and oft?

1.2. s.d. [and elsewhere] Calpurnia Calphurnia **3, 4, 6 Antonius', Antonius** Antonio's, Antonio [also l. 190 and 1.3.37] **24 s.d. Manent** Manet

1.3. 129 In Is

2.1. 40 ides first **67 of** of a **122 women, then,** women. Then **136 oath, when** Oath. When **214 eighth** eight **268 his** hit **281 the** tho **310 s.d. Enter Lucius** etc. [after "with haste" in l. 310 in F] **314 s.p. [and through l. 332] Ligarius** Cai

2.2. 23 did neigh do neigh **46 are** heare

2.3. 1 s.p. Artemidorus [not in F]

3.1. 40 law lane **114 states** State **116 lies** lye **256 s.p. Antony** [not in F] **277 s.d. Octavius'** Octauio's [also at 5.2.4] **285 for** from

3.2. 106 art are **205 s.p. All** [not in F] **222 wit** writ **260 s.d. Exeunt** Exit **262 s.d. Enter Servant** [after "fellow" in F]

4.2. 34–36 s.p. First, Second, Third Soldier [not in F] **50 Lucius** Lucillius **52 Lucilius** Lucius **s.d. Manent** Manet

4.3. 209 off off **230 s.d. Enter Lucius** [before l. 230 in F] **244, 246 [and throughout] Claudius** Claudio **246 [and throughout] Varro** Varrus **252 will** will it **303, 307 s.p. Varro, Claudius** Both

5.1. 42 teeth teethes **67 s.d. Exeunt** Exit **70** [F has s.d.: "Lucillius and Messala stand forth"] **71 s.p. Lucilius (Stands forth)** Luc **73 s.p. Messala (Stands forth)** Messa

5.3. 104 Thasos Tharsus **108 Flavius** Flauio

5.4. 7 s.p. Lucilius [not in F] **9 O** Luc. O **12, 15 s.p. First Soldier** Sold **16 s.d. Enter Antony** [before l. 16 in F] **17 the news** thee newes **30 whe'er** where

5.5. 77 With all Withall

Shakespeare's Sources

Julius Caesar represents Shakespeare's first extensive use of the work of the first-century Greek biographer Plutarch, in Thomas North's translation (based on the French, of Jacques Amyot) of *The Lives of the Noble Grecians and Romans* (1579 and 1595). Plutarch was to become Shakespeare's most often used source in the 1600s; prior to 1599 he had consulted it briefly on a number of other occasions. In *Julius Caesar*, he borrows details from three lives: Caesar, Brutus, and Antonius. He uses particular traits of character, such as Caesar's belief that it is "better to die once than always to be afraid of death," Brutus' determination to "frame his manners of life by the rules of virtue and study of philosophy," Cassius' choleric disposition and his "hating Caesar privately more than he did the tyranny openly," and Antonius' inclination to "rioting and banqueting."

The events of the play are substantially present in Plutarch, especially in "The Life of Julius Caesar" (as can be seen in the selection that follows). Antonius runs the course on the Feast of Lupercal to cure barrenness and offers the diadem to Caesar. Flavius and Marullus despoil the images of Caesar. Caesar observes that he mistrusts pale and lean men such as Brutus and Cassius. Papers are thrown by the conspirators where Brutus can find them, proclaiming "Thou sleepest, Brutus, and art not Brutus indeed." Caesar's death is preceded by prodigies: a slave's hand burns but is unconsumed, a sacrificial beast is found to contain no heart. When Caesar encounters the soothsayer who previously had warned him of his fate and boasts that "the ides of March be come," the soothsayer has the last word: "So be they, but yet are they not past." Brutus' wife Portia complains to him of being treated "like a harlot," not like a partner. Brutus commits what Plutarch calls two serious errors when he forbids his fellow conspirators to kill Antonius and when he permits Antonius to speak at Caesar's funeral. Cinna the Poet is slain by an angry crowd mistaking him for Cinna the conspirator. A ghost appears to Brutus shortly before the last battle saying, "I am thy ill angel, Brutus, and thou shalt see me by the city of Phillippes," to which Brutus replies, "Well, I shall see thee then." Antonius says of the vanquished conspirators that "there was none but Brutus only that was moved to do it, as thinking the act commendable of itself: but that all the other conspirators did conspire his death for some private malice or envy." Shakespeare's debt to Plutarch is greater than these few examples can indicate.

Of course Shakespeare reshapes and selects, as in his history plays. He compresses into one day Caesar's triumphant procession, the disrobing of the images, and the offer of the crown to Caesar on the Lupercal, when in fact these events were chronologically separate. Casca is by and large an invented character, and Octavius' role is considerably enlarged. Brutus' servant Lucius is a minor but effective addition, illustrating Brutus' capacity for warmth and humanity. Shakespeare accentuates the irrationality and vacillation of the mob, for in Plutarch the people are never much swayed by Brutus' rhetoric even though they respectfully allow him to speak. They are aroused to violence, in Plutarch's account, not by Antony's speech but by the revelation of Caesar's will and the sight of his mangled body. In fact, the unforgettable speeches of Brutus and Antony are not set down at all in Plutarch. More compression of time occurs after the assassination: in Plutarch, Octavius does not arrive in Rome until some six weeks afterward and does not agree to the formation of the Triumvirate until more than a year of quarreling has taken place. The inexorable buildup of tension in Shakespeare's play is the result of careful selection from a vast amount of material. Shakespeare's borrowing from "The Life of Marcus Brutus" is no less extensive and is at the same time reshaped and given new emphasis, as can be seen in the selection that follows.

Although Shakespeare depended heavily on Plutarch, he was also aware of later and conflicting traditions about Caesar. On the one hand, Dante's *Divine Comedy* (c. 1310–1321) consigns Brutus and Cassius to the lowest circle of hell along with Judas Iscariot and other betrayers of their masters. Geoffrey Chaucer's "The Monk's Tale," from the *Canterbury Tales*, similarly portrays Caesar as the manly and uncorruptible victim of envious attackers. On the other hand, Montaigne stresses the hubris of Caesar in aspiring to divinity. (Shakespeare could have read Montaigne in the French original, or, if he had access to a manuscript, in John Florio's English translation, published in 1603.) A pro-Brutus view could also be found in the Latin *Julius Caesar* of Marc-Antoine Muret (1553) and the French *César* of Jacques Grévin (1561). That Shakespeare knew these works is unlikely, but they kept alive a tradition with which he was certainly familiar. Possibly he knew such Roman works as Lucan's account of Caesar in the *Pharsalia* and Cicero's letters and orations, which were republican in tenor. Other possible sources include the *Chronicle of the Romans' Wars* by Appian of Alexandria (translated 1578), the anonymous play *Caesar's Revenge* (published 1606–1607, performed in the early 1590s at Oxford), and Thomas Kyd's *Cornelia* (translated from the French Senecan tragedy by Garnier). *Il Cesare* by Orlando Pescetti (1594) is now almost universally rejected as a possible source. The result of Shakespeare's acquaintance with both pro- and anti-Caesar traditions is that he subordinates his own political vision to a balanced presentation of history, showing the significant strengths and disabling weaknesses in both Caesar and the conspirators.

The Lives of the Noble Grecians and Romans Compared Together by . . . Plutarch

Translated by Thomas North

FROM THE LIFE OF JULIUS CAESAR

[Plutarch surveys the whole of Julius Caesar's early career: his first consulship, his conquests in Gaul and England, his crossing the Rubicon, his defeat of Pompey the Great at Pharsalia, his making Cleopatra Queen of Egypt, his *"Veni, vidi, vici,"* "I came, I saw, I conquered," after his victory over King Pharnaces, his being chosen perpetual dictator, and his enemies' resentment toward his growing power and ambition.]

But the chiefest cause that made him mortally hated was the covetous desire he had to be called king, which first gave the people just cause, and next his secret enemies honest color,[1] to bear him ill will. This notwithstanding, they that procured him this honor and dignity gave it out[2] among the people that it was written in the Sybilline prophecies how the Romans might overcome the Parthians if they made war with them and were led by a king, but otherwise that they[3] were unconquerable. And furthermore they[4] were so bold besides that, Caesar returning to Rome from the city of Alba, when they came to salute him, they called him king. But the people being offended, and Caesar also angry, he said he was not called king, but Caesar. Then every man keeping silence, he went his way heavy[5] and sorrowful.

When they had decreed divers honors for him in the Senate, the consuls and praetors, accompanied with[6] the whole assembly of the Senate, went unto him in the marketplace, where he was set by the pulpit for orations,[7] to tell him what honors they had decreed for him in his absence. But he, sitting still in his majesty, disdaining to rise up unto them when they came in, as if they had been private men, answered them that his honors had more need to be cut off

1 **color** excuse   2 **gave it out** let it be known   3 **they** i.e., the Parthians
4 **they** i.e., Caesar's supporters   5 **heavy** sad, pensive   6 **with** by   7 **was
set . . . orations** sat beside the pulpit used for public orations

than enlarged. This did not only offend the Senate but the common people also, to see that he should so lightly esteem of[8] the magistrates of the commonwealth, insomuch as every man that might lawfully go his way departed thence very sorrowfully. Thereupon also Caesar, rising, departed home to his house and, tearing open his doublet collar, making his neck bare, he cried out aloud to his friends that his throat was ready to offer to any man that would come and cut it. Notwithstanding it is reported that afterwards, to excuse this folly, he imputed it to his disease, saying that their wits are not perfect which have his disease of the falling evil[9] when, standing of their feet, they speak to the common people but are soon troubled with a trembling of their body and a sudden dimness and giddiness. But that was not true, for he would have risen up to the Senate, but Cornelius Balbus, one of his friends (but rather a flatterer), would not let him, saying: "What, do you not remember that you are Caesar, and will you not let them reverence you and do their duties?"

Besides these occasions[10] and offenses, there followed also his shame and reproach, abusing the tribunes of the people in this sort. At that time the feast Lupercalia was celebrated, the which in old time men say was the feast of shepherds or herdmen and is much like unto the feast of the Lycaeans in Arcadia. But howsoever it is, that day there are divers noblemen's sons, young men, and some of them magistrates themselves that govern then, which run naked through the city, striking in sport them they meet in their way with leather thongs, hair and all on, to make them give place.[11] And many noblewomen and gentlewomen also go of purpose[12] to stand in their way and do put forth their hands to be stricken, as scholars hold them out to their schoolmaster to be stricken with the ferula,[13] persuading themselves that, being[14] with child, they shall have good delivery, and also, being barren,[15] that it will make them to conceive with child. Caesar sat to behold that sport upon the pulpit for orations in a chair of gold, appareled in triumphing

---

8 esteem of esteem   **9 the falling evil** epilepsy   **10 occasions** grounds (for disapproval)   **11 give place** move out of the way   **12 of purpose** with intent   **13 ferula** cane or rod used as an instrument of punishment   **14 being** if they are   **15 also, being barren** and if they are barren

manner. Antonius, who was consul at that time, was one of them that ran this holy course. So when he came into the marketplace, the people made a lane for him to run at liberty,[16] and he came to Caesar and presented him a diadem wreathed about with laurel. Whereupon there rose a certain cry of rejoicing, not very great, done only by a few appointed[17] for the purpose. But when Caesar refused the diadem, then all the people together made an outcry of joy. Then Antonius offering it him again, there was a second shout of joy, but yet of a few. But when Caesar refused it again the second time, then all the whole people shouted. Caesar having made this proof[18] found that the people did not like of it, and thereupon rose out of his chair and commanded the crown to be carried unto Jupiter in the Capitol.

After that, there were set up images of Caesar in the city with diadems upon their heads, like kings. Those the two tribunes, Flavius and Marullus, went and pulled down, and furthermore, meeting with them that first saluted Caesar as king, they committed them to prison. The people followed them rejoicing at it and called them Brutes, because of Brutus who had in old time driven the kings out of Rome and that brought the kingdom of one person unto the government of the Senate and people. Caesar was so offended withal that he deprived Marullus and Flavius of their tribuneships, and accusing them, he spake also against the people and called them Bruti and Cumani, to wit, beasts and fools.

Hereupon the people went straight unto Marcus Brutus, who from his father came of[19] the first Brutus and by his mother of the house of the Servilians, a noble house as any was in Rome, and was also nephew and son-in-law of Marcus Cato. Notwithstanding, the great honors and favor Caesar showed unto him kept him back that of himself alone[20] he did not conspire nor consent to depose him of his kingdom. For Caesar did not only save[21] his life after the Battle of Pharsalia, when Pompey fled, and did at his request also save many more of his friends besides, but furthermore he put a marvelous confidence in him. For he had already pre-

16 at liberty where he wished   17 appointed agreed upon, designated
18 proof test   19 came of was descended from   20 that . . . alone so
that as far as he himself was concerned   21 save spare

ferred him[22] to the praetorship for that year and furthermore was[23] appointed to be consul the fourth year after
that, having through Caesar's friendship obtained it before
Cassius, who likewise made suit for the same; and Caesar
also, as it is reported, said in this contention, "Indeed Cassius hath alleged best reason, but yet shall he not be chosen
before Brutus." Some one day[24] accusing Brutus while he
practiced[25] this conspiracy, Caesar would not hear of it, but,
clapping his hand on his body, told them, "Brutus will look
for this skin"—meaning thereby that Brutus for his virtue
deserved to rule after him, but yet that, for ambition's sake,
he would not[26] show himself unthankful or dishonorable.

Now, they that desired change and wished Brutus only
their prince and governor above all other, they durst not
come to him themselves to tell him what they would have
him to do, but in the night did cast sundry papers into the
praetor's seat, where he gave audience, and the most of
them to this effect: "Thou sleepest, Brutus, and art not Brutus indeed." Cassius, finding Brutus' ambition stirred up
the more by these seditious bills,[27] did prick[28] him forward
and egg him on the more for a private quarrel he had conceived against Caesar, the circumstance whereof we have
set down more at large[29] in Brutus' life. Caesar also had
Cassius in great jealousy[30] and suspected him much, whereupon he said on a time[31] to his friends, "What will Cassius
do, think ye? I like not his pale looks." Another time when
Caesar's friends complained unto him of Antonius and Do-
labella, that they pretended[32] some mischief towards him,
he answered them again, "As for those fat men and smooth-
combed heads," quoth he, "I never reckon of them; but
these pale-visaged and carrion lean people, I fear them
most"—meaning Brutus and Cassius.

Certainly destiny may easier be foreseen than avoided,
considering the strange and wonderful[33] signs that were

---

22 **he had already preferred him** i.e., Caesar had already advanced or
promoted Brutus 23 **was** i.e., he, Brutus, was 24 **Some one day** one
day when some persons were 25 **practiced** plotted 26 **for
ambition's . . . not** he would not simply for ambition's sake 27 **bills**
letters, papers 28 **prick** spur 29 **at large** in detail 30 **had Cassius in
great jealousy** i.e., kept a wary eye on Cassius 31 **on a time** on one
occasion 32 **pretended** intended, plotted 33 **wonderful** wondrous

said to be seen before Caesar's death. For, touching the fires in the element[34] and spirits running up and down in the night, and also these solitary birds[35] to be seen at noondays sitting in the great marketplace, are not all these signs perhaps worth the noting, in such a wonderful chance as happened? But Strabo[36] the philosopher writeth that divers men were seen going up and down in fire, and furthermore that there was a slave of the soldiers that did cast a marvelous burning flame out of his hand, insomuch as they that saw it thought he had been burnt, but when the fire was out it was found he had no hurt. Caesar self[37] also, doing sacrifice unto the gods, found that one of the beasts which was sacrificed had no heart; and that was a strange thing in nature, how a beast could live without a heart.

Furthermore there was a certain soothsayer that had given Caesar warning long time afore to take heed of the day of the ides of March, which is the fifteenth of the month, for on that day he should be in great danger. That day being come, Caesar, going unto the Senate House and speaking merrily to the soothsayer, told him, "The ides of March be come." "So be they," softly answered the soothsayer, "but yet are they not past." And the very day before, Caesar, supping with Marcus Lepidus, sealed certain letters, as he was wont to do, at the board.[38] So, talk falling out amongst them[39] reasoning what death was best, he, preventing their opinions,[40] cried out aloud, "Death unlooked-for."

Then going to bed the same night, as his manner was, and lying with his wife Calpurnia, all the windows and doors of his chamber flying open, the noise awoke him and made him afraid when he saw such light, but more when he heard his wife Calpurnia, being fast asleep, weep and sigh and put forth many fumbling[41] lamentable speeches; for she dreamed that Caesar was slain and that she had him in her arms. Others also do deny that she had any such dream,[42]

---

34 touching . . . element as regards fires in the sky   35 these solitary birds i.e., owls   36 Strabo Stoic traveler and writer, c. 64 B.C.–A.D. 19   37 self himself   38 board dinner table   39 talk . . . them their talk happening to turn to the topic   40 preventing their opinions anticipating what they might say, speaking first   41 fumbling incoherent   42 do deny . . . dream i.e., deny that the dream took this particular form

as, amongst other, Titus Livius writeth that it was in this sort: the Senate having set upon the top of Caesar's house for an ornament and setting forth[43] of the same a certain pinnacle, Calpurnia dreamed that she saw it broken down and that she thought she lamented and wept for it. Insomuch that, Caesar rising in the morning, she prayed him if it were possible not to go out of the doors that day but to adjourn the session of the Senate until another day. And if that he made no reckoning of her dream, yet that he would search further of the soothsayers by their sacrifices to know what should happen him that day. Thereby it seemed that Caesar likewise did fear or suspect somewhat, because his wife Calpurnia until that time was never given to any fear or superstition and then for that[44] he saw her so troubled in mind with this dream she had. But much more afterwards, when the soothsayers, having sacrificed many beasts one after another, told him that none did like[45] them, then he determined to send Antonius to adjourn the session of the Senate.

But in the meantime came Decius Brutus, surnamed Albinus, in whom Caesar put such confidence that in his last will and testament he had appointed him to be his next heir, and yet was of the conspiracy with Cassius and Brutus. He, fearing that if Caesar did adjourn the session that day the conspiracy would be out, laughed the soothsayers to scorn and reproved Caesar, saying that he gave the Senate occasion to mislike with him[46] and that they might think he mocked them, considering that by his commandment they were assembled, and that they were ready willingly to grant him all things and to proclaim him king of all his provinces of the Empire of Rome out of Italy, and that he should wear his diadem in all other places both by sea and land. And furthermore that if any man should tell them from him they should[47] depart for that present time and return again when Calpurnia should have better dreams, what would his enemies and ill-willers[48] say and how could they like of[49] his friends' words? And who could persuade them otherwise

---

43 setting forth decorating   **44 for that** because   **45 like** satisfy, please   **46 mislike with him** disapprove of him   **47 tell . . . should** tell them as coming from Caesar that they, the Senators, were to   **48 ill-willers** evil-wishers   **49 like of** approve, believe, trust

but that they would think his dominion a slavery unto them and tyrannical in himself? "And yet if it be so," said he, "that you utterly mislike of[50] this day, it is better that you go yourself in person and, saluting the Senate, to dismiss them till another time." Therewithal he took Caesar by the hand and brought him out of his house.

Caesar was not gone far from his house but a bondman, a stranger, did what he could to speak with him; and when he saw he was put back by the great press and multitude of people that followed him, he went straight unto his house and put himself into Calpurnia's hands to be kept till Caesar came back again, telling her that he had great matters to impart unto him. And one Artemidorus also, born in the isle of Gnidos, a Doctor of Rhetoric in the Greek tongue, who by means of his profession was very familiar with certain of Brutus' confederates and therefore knew the most part of all their practices[51] against Caesar, came and brought him a little bill[52] written with his own hand of all that he meant to tell him. He, marking how Caesar received all the supplications that were offered him and that he gave them straight[53] to his men that were about him, pressed nearer to him and said: "Caesar, read this memorial[54] to yourself, and that quickly, for they be matters of great weight and touch you nearly." Caesar took it of him, but could never read it, though he many times attempted it, for the number of people that did salute him, but holding it still in his hand, keeping it to himself, went on withal into the Senate House. Howbeit others are of opinion that it was some man else that gave him that memorial and not Artemidorus, who did what he could all the way as he went to give it Caesar, but he was always repulsed by the people.

For these things, they may seem to come by chance;[55] but the place where the murder was prepared and where the Senate were assembled, and where also there stood up an image of Pompey dedicated by himself amongst other ornaments which he gave unto the theater—all these were manifest proofs that it was the ordinance of some god that made

50 mislike of disapprove of, mistrust   **51 practices** conspiracies   **52 bill** memorandum   **53 straight** immediately   **54 memorial** memorandum **55 For these . . . chance** as for these things, they may seem to occur merely by chance

this treason to be executed specially in that very place. It is also reported that Cassius, though otherwise he did favor the doctrine of Epicurus, beholding the image of Pompey before they entered into the action of their traitorous enterprise, he did softly call upon it to aid him; but the instant danger of the present time, taking away his former reason, did suddenly put him into a furious passion and made him like a man half beside himself.

Now Antonius, that was a faithful friend to Caesar and a valiant man besides of his hands,[56] him Decius Brutus Albinus entertained out of[57] the Senate House, having begun a long tale of set purpose.[58] So Caesar coming into the house, all the Senate stood up on their feet to do him honor. Then part of Brutus' company and confederates stood round about Caesar's chair, and part of them also came towards him as though they made suit with Metellus Cimber to call home his brother again from banishment. And thus prosecuting still their suit, they followed Caesar till he was set in his chair. Who, denying their petitions and being offended with them one after another because the more they were denied the more they pressed upon him and were the earnester with him, Metellus at length, taking his gown with both his hands, pulled it over his neck, which was the sign given the confederates to set upon him.

Then Casca, behind him, strake him[59] in the neck with his sword. Howbeit the wound was not great nor mortal, because it seemed the fear of such a devilish attempt did amaze him[60] and take his strength from him, that he killed him not at the first blow. But Caesar, turning straight unto him, caught hold of his sword and held it hard; and they both cried out, Caesar in Latin: "O vile traitor Casca, what dost thou?" and Casca, in Greek, to his brother: "Brother, help me!" At the beginning of this stir, they that were present, not knowing of the conspiracy, were so amazed with the horrible sight they saw that they had no power to fly, neither to help him nor so much as once to make an outcry. They on the other side that had conspired his death com-

---

56 of his hands i.e., with his weapons, in hand-to-hand combat
57 entertained out of engaged, held in conversation outside of   **58 of**
set purpose devised for the occasion   **59 strake him** i.e., struck Caesar
60 amaze him i.e., dazzle Casca

passed him in on every side with their swords drawn in their hands, that Caesar turned him nowhere but he was stricken at by some and still had naked swords in his face, and was hacked and mangled among them as[61] a wild beast taken of[62] hunters. For it was agreed among them that every man should give him a wound, because all their parts should be[63] in this murder. And then Brutus himself gave him one wound about his privities. Men report also that Caesar did still[64] defend himself against the rest, running every way with his body; but when he saw Brutus with his sword drawn in his hand, then he pulled his gown over his head and made no more resistance, and was driven either casually or purposedly[65] by the counsel of the conspirators against the base whereupon Pompey's image stood, which ran all of a gore blood[66] till he was slain. Thus it seemed that the image took just revenge of Pompey's enemy, being thrown down on the ground at his feet and yielding up his ghost there for[67] the number of wounds he had upon him. For it is reported that he had three-and-twenty wounds upon his body; and divers of the conspirators did hurt themselves, striking one body with so many blows.

When Caesar was slain, the Senate (though Brutus stood in the midst amongst them, as though he would have said something touching this fact[68]) presently[69] ran out of the house and, flying, filled all the city with marvelous[70] fear and tumult. Insomuch as some did shut to their doors, others forsook their shops and warehouses, and others ran to the place to see what the matter was; and others also that had seen it ran home to their houses again. But Antonius and Lepidus, which were two of Caesar's chiefest friends, secretly conveying themselves away, fled into other men's houses and forsook their own.

Brutus and his confederates on the other side, being yet hot with this murder they had committed, having their swords drawn in their hands, came all in a troop together out of the Senate and went into the marketplace, not as men

61 as like **62 of** by **63 all their parts should be** they should all take part **64 still** continually **65 purposedly** purposely **66 of a gore blood** all covered with blood **67 for** because of **68 fact** deed **69 presently** immediately **70 marvelous** inspired by astonishment and the supernatural

that made countenance to fly, but otherwise[71] boldly holding up their heads like men of courage, and called to the
people to defend their liberty, and stayed to speak with
every great personage whom they met in their way. Of them,
some followed this troop and went amongst them as if they
had been of the conspiracy, and falsely challenged[72] part of
the honor with them; among them was Caius Octavius
and Lentulus Spinther. But both of them were afterwards
put to death for their vain covetousness of honor by Antonius and Octavius Caesar the younger, and yet had no part
of that honor for the which they were put to death,
neither did any man believe that they were any of the confederates or of counsel with them. For they that did put
them to death took revenge rather of the will they had to
offend[73] than of any fact[74] they had committed.

The next morning Brutus and his confederates came into
the marketplace to speak unto the people, who gave them
such audience that it seemed they neither greatly reproved
nor allowed the fact;[75] for by their great silence they showed
that they were sorry for Caesar's death and also that they
did reverence Brutus. Now, the Senate granted general pardon for all that was past, and to pacify every man ordained
besides that Caesar's funerals should be honored as a god,[76]
and established[77] all things that he had done, and gave certain provinces also and convenient honors unto Brutus and
his confederates, whereby every man thought all things
were brought to good peace and quietness again.

But when they had opened Caesar's testament[78] and
found a liberal legacy of money bequeathed unto every citizen of Rome, and that[79] they saw his body (which was
brought into the marketplace) all bemangled[80] with gashes
of swords, then there was no order to keep the multitude
and common people quiet, but they plucked up forms,[81] ta-

---

71 made countenance to fly, but otherwise looked as though they were
about to flee, but to the contrary   **72 challenged** claimed   **73 of the
will . . . offend** i.e., for their having wanted to be part of the conspiracy
74 fact deed   **75 allowed the fact** approved of the deed   **76 as a god** as
if he were a god   **77 established** enacted permanently   **78 testament**
will   **79 that** i.e., when   **80 bemangled** mangled   **81 forms** benches

bles, and stools and laid them all about the body and, setting them afire, burnt the corpse. Then when the fire was well kindled, they took the firebrands and went unto their houses that had slain Caesar to set them afire.[82] Other[83] also ran up and down the city to see if they could meet with any of them to cut them in pieces; howbeit, they could meet with never a man of them because they had locked themselves up safely in their houses.

There was one of Caesar's friends called Cinna that had a marvelous strange and terrible dream the night before. He dreamed that Caesar bade him to supper and that he refused and would not go; then that Caesar took him by the hand and led him against his will. Now Cinna, hearing at that time that they burnt Caesar's body in the marketplace, notwithstanding that he feared his dream and had an ague on him besides, he went into the marketplace to honor his funerals. When he came thither, one of the mean sort[84] asked what his name was. He was straight called by his name. The first man told it to another and that other unto another, so that it ran straight through them all that he was one of them that murdered Caesar; for indeed one of the traitors to Caesar was also called Cinna as[85] himself. Wherefore taking him for Cinna the murderer they fell upon him with such fury that they presently dispatched him in the marketplace.

This stir and fury made Brutus and Cassius more afraid than of all that was past,[86] and therefore within few days after[87] they departed out of Rome. And touching their doings afterwards, and what calamity they suffered till their deaths, we have written it at large in the life of Brutus. Caesar died at six-and-fifty years of age, and Pompey also lived not passing[88] four years more than he. So he reaped no other fruit of all his reign and dominion, which he had so vehemently desired all his life and pursued with such extreme danger, but a vain name only and a superficial glory that procured him the envy and hatred of his country.

But his great prosperity and good fortune that favored

---

82 **went . . . afire** went to the houses of those who had slain Caesar and set those houses afire   83 **Other** others   84 **of the mean sort** of lower station   85 **as** like   86 **was past** was happening, had happened   87 **after** afterward   88 **passing** exceeding

him all his lifetime did continue afterwards in the revenge
of his death, pursuing the murderers both by sea and land
till they had not left a man more to be executed of all them
that were actors or counselors in the conspiracy of his
death. Furthermore, of all the chances that happen unto
men upon the earth, that which came to Cassius above all
other is most to be wondered at; for he, being overcome in
battle at the journey of Philippes, slew himself with the
same sword with the which he strake[89] Caesar. Again, of
signs in the element[90] the great comet, which seven nights
together was seen very bright after Caesar's death, the
eighth night after was never seen more. Also the brightness
of the sun was darkened, the which all that year through
rose very pale and shined not out, whereby it gave but small
heat; therefore the air being very cloudy and dark, by the
weakness of the heat that could not come forth, did cause
the earth to bring forth but raw and unripe fruit which rot-
ted before it could ripe.

But above all, the ghost that appeared unto Brutus
showed plainly that the gods were offended with the murder of Caesar. The vision was thus: Brutus, being ready to
pass over his army from the city of Abydos to the other
coast lying directly against it,[91] slept every night as his manner was in his tent; and being yet awake, thinking of his affairs (for by report he was as careful a captain[92] and lived
with as little sleep as ever man did), he thought he heard a
noise at his tent door, and looking towards the light of the
lamp that waxed very dim, he saw a horrible vision of a
man, of a wonderful[93] greatness and dreadful look, which at
the first made him marvelously afraid. But when he saw
that it did him no hurt but stood by his bedside and said
nothing, at length he asked him what he was. The image answered him: "I am thy ill angel, Brutus, and thou shalt see
me by the city of Philippes." Then Brutus replied again and
said, "Well, I shall see thee then." Therewithal the spirit
presently[94] vanished from him.

After that time Brutus, being in battle near unto the city

---

89 strake struck   **90 element** sky, heavens   **91 against it** opposite it
(across the Hellespont)   **92 as careful a captain** as watchful and attentive to duty a commanding officer   **93 wonderful** wondrous   **94 presently** immediately

of Philippes against Antonius and Octavius Caesar, at the first battle he wan[95] the victory, and overthrowing all them that withstood him he drave[96] them into young Caesar's camp, which he took. The second battle being at hand, this spirit appeared again unto him but spake never a word. Thereupon Brutus, knowing he should die, did put himself to all hazard in battle, but yet fighting could not be slain. So seeing his men put to flight and overthrown, he ran unto a little rock not far off and there, setting his sword's point to his breast, fell upon it and slew himself; but yet, as it is reported, with the help of his friend that dispatched him.

Text based on *The Lives of the Noble Grecians and Romans Compared Together by That Grave, Learned Philosopher and Historiographer, Plutarch of Chaeronea. Translated out of Greek into French by James Amyot . . . and out of French into English by Thomas North. . . . Thomas Vautroullier . . . 1579.*

95 wan won   **96 drave** drove

The Lives of the Noble Grecians and Romans Compared Together by . . . Plutarch
Translated by Thomas North

FROM THE LIFE OF MARCUS BRUTUS

[After the assassination of Julius Caesar, the triumvirs, Octavius Caesar, Antonius, and Lepidus, divide the Empire of Rome among themselves. Brutus and Cassius meanwhile take their armies into the Middle East, forming alliances and gathering support for their cause. Friction develops between them over Brutus' concern that Cassius is too ready to conquer for his own glory and profit when their only purpose ought to be to free Italy from the dictatorship of the triumvirs. The nations that yield to Brutus, such as the Patareians, find themselves humanely treated.]

So after they had thus yielded themselves, divers other cities also followed them and did the like, and found Brutus more merciful and courteous than they thought they should have done, but specially far above Cassius. For Cassius, about the selfsame time, after he had compelled the Rhodians every man to deliver all the ready money they had in gold and silver in their houses, the which being brought together amounted to the sum of eight thousand talents, yet he condemned the city besides to pay the sum of five hundred talents more. Where Brutus, in contrary manner, after he had levied of all the country of Lycia but a hundred and fifty talents only, he departed thence into the country of Ionia and did them no more hurt. Now Brutus in all this journey did many notable acts and worthy of memory, both for rewarding as also in punishing those that had deserved it. . . .

About that time, Brutus sent to pray Cassius to come to the city of Sardis, and so he did. Brutus, understanding of his coming, went to meet him with all his friends. There, both their armies being armed, they called them both emperors. Now, as it commonly happeneth in great affairs between two persons, both of them having many friends and so many captains under them, there ran tales and com-

plaints betwixt them. Therefore, before they fell in hand
with[1] any other matter, they went into a little chamber together, and bade every man avoid[2] and did shut the doors to
them. Then they began to pour out their complaints one to
the other and grew hot and loud, earnestly accusing one another, and at length fell both a-weeping. Their friends that
were without[3] the chamber, hearing them loud within and
angry between themselves, they were both amazed and
afraid also lest it would grow to further matter. But yet they
were commanded that no man should come to them.

Notwithstanding, one Marcus Phaonius, that had been a
friend and follower of Cato[4] while he lived and took upon
him to counterfeit a philosopher—not with wisdom and dis-
cretion, but with a certain bedlam[5] and frantic motion—he
would needs[6] come into the chamber, though the men offered[7] to keep him out. But it was no boot to let[8] Phaonius
when a mad mood or toy[9] took him in the head, for he was a
hot, hasty man and sudden in all his doings, and cared for
never a senator of them all. Now, though he used this bold
manner of speech after the profession of the Cynic philosophers[10] (as who would say,[11] dogs)[12] yet this boldness did no
hurt many times, because they did but laugh at him to see
him so mad. This Phaonius at that time, in despite of the
doorkeepers, came into the chamber, and with a certain
scoffing and mocking gesture, which he counterfeited of
purpose,[13] he rehearsed[14] the verses which old Nestor said
in Homer:

My lords, I pray you, hearken both to me,
For I have seen more years than such ye three.

Cassius fell a-laughing at him, but Brutus thrust him out of

1 **fell in hand with** took up   2 **avoid** go out of the room   3 **without**
outside   4 **Cato** Roman philosopher, 231–149 B.C., who opposed extrava-
gance and luxury, advocating a return to primitive agricultural simplic-
ity   5 **bedlam** mad   6 **would needs** felt it necessary that he, took
it upon himself to   7 **offered** attempted   8 **no boot to let** useless to
hinder   9 **toy** whim   10 **profession of the Cynic philosophers** practice
or custom among those philosophers known as Cynics (among whose
chief tenets was the despising of ease, riches, and fleshly indulgence)
11 **as who would say** as one might say   12 **dogs** (*Cynic* is derived from
the Greek *kunikos*, doglike, currish. Diogenes, the famous Cynic of the
fourth century B.C., was renowned for his snarling and biting criticism.)
13 **of purpose** on purpose   14 **rehearsed** recited

the chamber and called him dog and counterfeit Cynic.
Howbeit his coming in brake their strife at that time, and so
they left each other.

The selfsame night, Cassius prepared his supper in his
chamber, and Brutus brought his friends with him. So
when they were set at supper, Phaonius came to sit down
after he had washed. Brutus told him aloud no man sent for
him, and bade them set him at the upper end—meaning indeed at the lower end of the bed. Phaonius made no ceremony but thrust in amongst the midst of them and made
all the company laugh at him. So they were merry all suppertime and full of their philosophy.

The next day after, Brutus, upon complaint of the Sardians, did condemn and noted[15] Lucius Pella for a defamed
person—that had been a praetor of the Romans and whom
Brutus had given charge[16] unto—for that he was accused
and convicted of robbery and pilfery in his office. This judgment much misliked[17] Cassius, because he himself had secretly (not many days before) warned two of his friends
attainted[18] and convicted of the like offenses and openly
had cleared them; but yet he did not therefore leave[19] to em-
ploy them in any manner of service as he did before. And
therefore he greatly reproved Brutus for that he would
show himself so straight[20] and severe in such a time as was
meeter to bear a little[21] than to take things at the worst.

Brutus in contrary manner answered that he should remember the ides of March, at which time they slew Julius
Caesar, who neither pilled nor polled[22] the country but only
was a favorer and suborner[23] of all them that did rob and
spoil by his countenance and authority.[24] And if there were
any occasion whereby they might honestly set aside justice
and equity, they should have had more reason to have suffered[25] Caesar's friends to have robbed and done what
wrong and injury they had would than to bear with[26] their

15 noted publicly disgraced. (See *Julius Caesar*, 4.3.2.) **16 charge**
authority **17 misliked** displeased **18 attainted** i.e., charged **19 leave**
refrain, leave off **20 straight** rigid **21 as was meeter . . . little** i.e.,
when it was more suitable to be a little indulgent **22 pilled nor polled**
plundered nor pillaged. (The words are synonymous.) **23 suborner**
encourager, one who aids and commissions **24 countenance and
authority** (Synonymous terms.) **25 suffered** allowed **26 they had
would . . . bear with** they had intended than to excuse, tolerate the
conduct of

own men. "For then," said he, "they[27] could but have said they[28] had been cowards;[29] and now they may accuse us of injustice, besides the pains we take and the danger we put ourselves into." And thus may we see what Brutus' intent and purpose was.

But as they both prepared to pass over again out of Asia into Europe, there went a rumor that there appeared a wonderful[30] sign unto him. Brutus was a careful[31] man and slept very little, both for that his diet was moderate as also because he was continually occupied. He never slept in the daytime, and in the night no longer than the time he was driven[32] to be alone and when everybody else took their rest. But now, whilst he was in war and his head ever busily occupied to think of his affairs and what would happen, after he had slumbered a little after supper he spent all the rest of the night in dispatching of his weightiest causes; and after he had taken order for them, if he had any leisure left him, he would read some book till the third watch of the night, at what time the captains, petty captains, and colonels did use to come unto him.

So, being ready to go into Europe, one night very late (when all the camp took quiet rest) as he was in his tent with a little light, thinking of weighty matters, he thought he heard one come in to him and, casting his eye towards the door of his tent, that[33] he saw a wonderful strange and monstrous shape of a body coming towards him and said never a word. So Brutus boldly asked what he was, a god or a man, and what cause brought him thither. The spirit answered him, "I am thy evil spirit, Brutus, and thou shalt see me by the city of Philippes." Brutus, being no otherwise afraid, replied again unto it: "Well, then I shall see thee again." The spirit presently vanished away, and Brutus called his men unto him, who told him that they heard no noise nor saw anything at all. Thereupon Brutus returned again to think on his matters as he did before.

And when the day brake, he went unto Cassius to tell him what vision had appeared unto him in the night. Cassius,

27 **they** i.e., people   28 **they** i.e., Brutus and Cassius   29 **cowards** i.e.,
for not standing up bravely to corruption   30 **wonderful** portentous
31 **careful** full of cares, watchful, attentive to duty   32 **driven** obliged
33 **that** i.e., he thought that

being in opinion an Epicurean[34] and reasoning thereon with Brutus, spake to him touching the vision thus: "In our sect, Brutus, we have an opinion that we do not always feel or see that which we suppose we do both see and feel, but that our senses, being credulous and therefore easily abused (when they are idle and unoccupied in their own objects), are induced to imagine they see and conjecture that which they in truth do not. For our mind is quick and cunning to work, without either cause or matter, anything in the imagination whatsoever. And therefore the imagination is resembled to clay and the mind to the potter who, without any other cause than his fancy and pleasure, changeth it into what fashion and form he will. And this doth the diversity of our dreams show unto us. For our imagination doth upon a small fancy grow from conceit[35] to conceit, altering both in passions and forms of things imagined. For the mind of man is ever occupied, and that continual moving[36] is nothing but an imagination.

"But yet there is a further cause of this in you. For, you being by nature given to melancholic discoursing and of late continually occupied, your wits and senses, having been overlabored, do easilier yield to such imaginations. For to say that there are spirits or angels and, if there were, that they had the shape of men, or such voices, or any power at all to come unto us, it is a mockery. And for mine own part I would there were such, because that we should not only have soldiers, horses, and ships but also the aid of the gods to guide and further our honest and honorable attempts." With these words Cassius did somewhat comfort and quiet Brutus.

When they raised[37] their camp, there came two eagles that, flying with a marvelous force, lighted upon two of the foremost ensigns[38] and always followed the soldiers, which[39] gave them meat and fed them until they came near to the city of Philippes. And there, one day only before the battle, they both flew away.

---

34 Epicurean one who maintains that there is nothing to fear from God and nothing to feel in death, that a good life of plain living and virtue is attainable, and that good is knowable only by the senses as an absence of pain **35 conceit** notion, idea **36 that continual moving** the continual motion of the mind **37 raised** struck, ended, took down **38 ensigns** standards **39 which** who

Now Brutus had conquered the most part of all the people and nations of that country; but if there were[40] any other city or captain to overcome, then they made all clear before them and so drew towards the coasts of Thasos. There Norbanus,[41] lying in camp in a certain place called the straits by[42] another place called Symbolon (which is a port of the sea), Cassius and Brutus compassed him in[43] in such sort that he was driven to forsake the place which was of great strength for him, and he was also in danger besides to have lost all his army. For Octavius Caesar could not follow him[44] because of his[45] sickness and therefore stayed behind, whereupon they had taken his army had not Antonius' aid been,[46] which made such wonderful speed that Brutus could scant believe it. So Caesar came not thither of[47] ten days after; and Antonius camped against Cassius and Brutus on the other side against Caesar.

The Romans called the valley between both camps the Philippian fields; and there were never seen two so great armies of the Romans, one before[48] the other, ready to fight. In truth, Brutus' army was inferior to Octavius Caesar's in number of men, but for bravery[49] and rich furniture[50] Brutus' army far excelled Caesar's. For the most part of their armors were silver and gilt, which Brutus had bountifully given them, although in all other things he taught his captains to live in order without excess. But for the bravery of armor and weapon which soldiers should carry in their hands or otherwise wear upon their backs, he thought that it was an encouragement unto them that by nature are greedy of honor, and that it maketh them also fight like devils that love to get[51] and be afraid to lose, because they fight to keep their armor and weapon as also their goods and lands.

Now when they came to muster their armies, Octavius Caesar took the muster of his army within the trenches of

---

40 if there were i.e., in case there were   **41 Norbanus** a Roman general of the triumvirate stationed at *Thasos,* an island in the northern Aegean off the coast of northeast Greece   **42 by** nearby   **43 compassed him in** surrounded him   **44 follow him** i.e., follow with support for Norbanus   **45 his** i.e., Caesar's   **46 had not Antonius' aid been** had it not been for Antonius' aid   **47 came not thither of** did not arrive there until   **48 before** facing, in front of   **49 bravery** splendor   **50 furniture** equipment   **51 get** acquire

his camp and gave his men only a little corn and five silver drachmas to every man to sacrifice to the gods and to pray for victory. But Brutus, scorning this misery[52] and niggardliness, first of all mustered his army and did purify it in the fields according to the manner of the Romans, and then he gave unto every band a number of wethers[53] to sacrifice and fifty silver drachmas to every soldier. So that Brutus' and Cassius' soldiers were better pleased and more courageously bent to fight at the day of the battle than their enemies' soldiers were.

Notwithstanding, being busily occupied about the ceremonies of this purification, it is reported that there chanced certain unlucky signs unto Cassius. For one of his sergeants that carried the rods[54] before him brought him the garland of flowers turned backwards, the which he should have worn[55] on his head in the time of sacrificing. Moreover, it is reported also that at another time before, in certain sports and triumphs[56]* where they carried an image of Cassius' victory of clean[57] gold, it fell by chance, the man stumbling that carried it. And yet further, there were seen a marvelous number of fowls of prey that feed upon dead carcasses, and beehives also were found where bees were gathered together in a certain place within the trenches of the camp—the which place the soothsayers thought good to shut out of the precinct of the camp for to[58] take away the superstitious fear and mistrust men would have of it. The which began somewhat to alter Cassius' mind from Epicurus' opinions and had put the soldiers also in a marvelous fear.

Thereupon Cassius was of opinion not to try this war at one battle but rather to delay time and to draw it out in length, considering that they were the stronger in money and the weaker in men and armors. But Brutus in contrary manner did alway before, and at that time also, desire nothing more than to put all to the hazard of battle as soon as might be possible, to the end he might either quickly re-

52 misery wretchedness, privation 53 wethers male sheep 54 rods fasces, bundles of rods with a projecting ax blade, borne ceremoniously before Roman magistrates and dignitaries as a badge of authority 55 he should have worn i.e., Cassius was to have worn 56 triumphs victory celebrations 57 clean pure 58 for to in order to

store his country to her former liberty or rid him[59] forth-
with of this miserable world, being still troubled in
following and maintaining of such great armies together.
But perceiving that in the daily skirmishes and bickerings[60]
they made his men were alway the stronger and ever had
the better, that[61] yet quickened his spirits again and did put
him in better heart. And furthermore, because that some of
their own men had already yielded themselves to their enemies and that it was suspected moreover divers others
would do the like, that[62] made many of Cassius' friends,
which were of his mind before, when it came to be debated
in council whether the battle should be fought or not, that
they were then of Brutus' mind.

But yet was there one of Brutus' friends called Atellius
that was against it and was of opinion that they should
tarry the next winter. Brutus asked him what he should get
by tarrying a year longer? "If I get naught else," quoth Atellius again, "yet have I lived so much longer." Cassius was
very angry with this answer, and Atellius was maliced[63] and
esteemed the worse for it of all men. Thereupon it was presently determined they should fight battle the next day. So
Brutus all suppertime looked with a cheerful countenance,
like a man that had good hope, and talked very wisely of
philosophy and after supper went to bed.

But touching Cassius, Messala reporteth that he supped
by himself in his tent with a few of his friends and that all
suppertime he looked very sadly and was full of thoughts,
although it was against his nature; and that after supper he
took him by the hand and, holding him fast, in token of
kindness as his manner was, told him in Greek: "Messala, I
protest unto thee and make thee my witness that I am compelled against my mind and will, as Pompey the Great was,
to jeopard[64] the liberty of our country to the hazard of a
battle. And yet we must be lively and of good courage, considering our good fortune, whom we should wrong too
much to mistrust her, although we follow evil counsel."[65]

---

59 rid him rid himself   **60 bickerings** skirmishes   **61 that** that realiza-
tion   **62 that** that consideration   **63 maliced** scorned   **64 jeopard**
jeopardize   **65 although . . . counsel** i.e., even if we are obliged to follow
Brutus' bad advice and fight inopportunely

Messala writeth that Cassius, having spoken these last words unto him, he bade him farewell and willed him to come to supper to him the next night following because it was his birthday.

The next morning, by break of day, the signal of battle was set out in Brutus' and Cassius' camp, which was an arming[66] scarlet coat. And both the chieftains spake together in the midst of their armies. There Cassius began to speak first and said: "The gods grant us, O Brutus, that this day we may win the field, and ever after to live all the rest of our life quietly, one with another. But sith[67] the gods have so ordained it that the greatest and chiefest things amongst men are most uncertain, and that if the battle fall out otherwise today than we wish or look for, we shall hardly meet again. What art thou then determined to do, to fly, or die?" Brutus answered him, being yet but a young man and not overgreatly experienced in the world: "I trust (I know not how) a certain rule of philosophy, by the which I did greatly blame and reprove Cato for killing of himself, as being no lawful nor godly act touching the gods nor concerning men valiant, not to give place and yield to divine providence and not constantly and patiently to take whatsoever it pleaseth him[68] to send us but to draw back, and fly.[69] But being now in the midst of the danger, I am of a contrary mind. For if it be not the will of God that this battle fall out fortunate for us, I will look no more for hope, neither seek to make any new supply for war again, but will rid me of this miserable world and content me with my fortune. For I gave up my life for my country in the ides of March, for the which I shall live in another more glorious world." Cassius fell a-laughing to hear what he said and, embracing him, "Come on, then," said he, "let us go and charge our enemies with this mind. For either we shall conquer or we shall not need to fear the conquerors."

---

66 arming providing protective covering for the body **67 sith** since
68 him i.e., God **69 fly** flee

[The events of the battle, and of Cassius' and Brutus' suicides, are essentially as in Shakespeare's play.]

Text based on *The Lives of the Noble Grecians and Romans Compared Together by That Grave, Learned Philosopher and Historiographer, Plutarch of Chaeronea. Translated out of Greek into French by James Amyot . . . and out of French into English by Thomas North. . . . Thomas Vautroullier . . . 1579.*

In the following, the departure from the original text appears in boldface; the original reading is in roman.

p. 127 **triumphs** triumphe

Further Reading

Berry, Ralph. "Communal Identity and the Rituals of *Julius Caesar.*" *Shakespeare and the Awareness of the Audience.* New York: St. Martin's Press, 1985. Berry finds the roots of the play's tragic action not in individual character but in a "communal identity" derived from the city itself: Rome is "the social determinant of the action." When characters express individuality they do so in response to pressures generated by the city, forcing them into archaic roles that are played out with a "diminishing expectation of success" and are effective only in "the mastering of defeat."

Bonjour, Adrien. *The Structure of "Julius Caesar."* Liverpool, Eng.: Liverpool Univ. Press, 1958. Bonjour explores the antithetical structure of the play and its careful balance of sympathy, "perfectly divided between the victim of the crime and the victim of the punishment." Imagery and characterization confirm the ambivalence of the plotting, deepening the agnostic political vision.

Burckhardt, Sigurd. "How Not to Murder Caesar." *Shakespearean Meanings.* Princeton, N.J.: Princeton Univ. Press, 1968. Likening the conspiracy to a dramatic plot, Burckhardt discovers in the failure of Brutus' political design a series of aesthetic misjudgments. Brutus would fashion the assassination as a "classical, almost Aristotelian" tragedy to be played before "an audience of noble, sturdy republicans," but his assumptions about the appropriate political style are wrong for the reality of imperial Rome.

Burke, Kenneth. "Antony in Behalf of the Play." *Southern Review* 1 (1935): 308–319. Rpt. in *The Philosophy of Literary Form*. Baton Rouge, La.: Louisiana State Univ. Press, 1941. Burke constructs a speech by a garrulous Antony directed not at the Roman populace but at the audience of *Julius Caesar*, explaining the play's "mechanism and its virtues." Burke's Antony exposes the rhetorical manipulations of Shakespeare's play that make the audience complicit in Caesar's murder and then desirous of Brutus' death to "absolve" them of their guilt.

Charney, Maurice. "The Imagery of *Julius Caesar*." *Shake-*

speare's Roman Plays: The Function of Imagery in the Drama. Cambridge: Harvard Univ. Press, 1961. Charney's analysis reveals the centrality and ambivalence of the play's imagery of fire, blood, and storms. The ambiguity serves Shakespeare's interest in exploring, rather than arbitrating, conflicting political claims that would have been "of lively contemporary interest."

Daiches, David. *Shakespeare: "Julius Caesar."* London: Edward Arnold, 1976. In an essay designed to introduce the play to students, Daiches examines the unfolding action, tracing Shakespeare's control of his audience's response. The moral balances of the play are delicately maintained: Brutus appears at once idealistic and naive; Caesar, proud and frail. The play's only absolute resides in the grim efficiency of the new political ruler, Octavius.

Doran, Madeleine. " 'What should be in that "Caesar"?': Proper Names in *Julius Caesar.*" *Shakespeare's Dramatic Language*. Madison, Wis.: Univ. of Wisconsin Press, 1976. Doran notes Shakespeare's unusual emphasis on names in the play and examines how the sounded names establish the tension between the paired protagonists. Only with Antony's eulogy does the disjunction end "between Brutus and Caesar which Cassius began in setting their names against one another."

Mack, Maynard. *"Julius Caesar."* In *Modern Shakespearean Criticism: Essays on Style, Dramaturgy, and the Major Plays*, ed. Alvin B. Kernan. New York: Harcourt, Brace and World, 1970. Mack finds the play's theme in "the always ambiguous impact between man and history." The first half of the play focuses on the efforts of characters to exert their wills upon history, but the second half shows "the insufficiency of reason and rational expectation." Brutus fails because his idealism prevents him from seeing history's limited responsiveness to human influence: he successfully kills Caesar but the spirit he would destroy "must repeatedly be killed but never dies."

Ornstein, Robert. "Seneca and the Political Drama of *Julius Caesar.*" *Journal of English and Germanic Philology* 57 (1958): 51–56. Ornstein discovers in Seneca's *De Beneficiis* a perspective for understanding Brutus' political role, one that lends support to modern ironic readings of the play. Following Seneca, "Shakespeare realizes that the essential drama of Brutus' role in the conspiracy lay not in a conflict of republican and monarchal theories" (for Brutus lacks a clearly defined political ideology) but in a "tragic disparity between naïve illusions and political realities."

Prior, Moody E. "The Search for a Hero in *Julius Caesar*." *Renaissance Drama* n.s. 2 (1969): 81–101. Prior examines the play's structure and finds that it is neither the tragedy of Julius Caesar nor of Brutus. The play is not organized around a single character but, like the *Henry IV* plays, divides its action among several characters and takes its name from a "central figure" in relation to whom events find meaning. The play's treatment of politics, however, is more like the treatment in the tragedies, with a focus on moral rather than historical implications.

Rabkin, Norman. "Structure, Convention, and Meaning in *Julius Caesar*." *Journal of English and Germanic Philology* 63 (1964): 240–254. Rpt. rev. in *Shakespeare and the Common Understanding*. New York: Free Press, 1967. The clear parallels that Rabkin sees between Caesar and Brutus establish the assassination as a "criminal mistake" rather than an "act of public virtue." Antony's speech in the forum declares the failure of Brutus' "naive idealization" of the murder of Caesar and marks a change of course in the drama that is virtually a shift in dramatic convention: Shakespeare turns "what promised to be a tragical history into a revenge play" that reveals the limits of human will and desire.

Ripley, John. *"Julius Caesar" on Stage in England and America, 1599–1973*. Cambridge and New York: Cambridge Univ. Press, 1980. Ripley provides a history of *Julius Caesar* on the stage, as it has diversely served as a "star-vehicle," a "clothes-horse for pageantry," and as a "political medium." His discussion of distinctive productions includes textual changes, stagecraft, and the interpretation of character.

Schanzer, Ernest. "The Tragedy of Shakespeare's Brutus." *ELH* 22 (1955): 1–15. Rpt. rev. in *The Problem Plays of Shakespeare: A Study of "Julius Caesar," "Measure for Measure," and "Antony and Cleopatra."* New York:

Schocken, 1963. Schanzer discusses "the complex and divided attitude to the Caesar story found in Shakespeare's play" and in his sources, and proposes that Shakespeare is less interested in deciding whether or not the assassination is justifiable than in exploring the moral questions to which it gives rise. The denial to an audience of secure "moral bearings" establishes *Julius Caesar* as one of Shakespeare's "genuine problem plays."

Shaw, George Bernard. *"Julius Caesar." Shaw on Shakespeare,* ed. Edwin Wilson. New York: E. P. Dutton, 1961. Shaw is perhaps the most virulent detractor of Shakespeare's handling of the play's political conflict. Declaring that his "truce with Shakespeare is over," Shaw is contemptuous of Shakespeare's "travestying" of Caesar as "a silly braggart" and of the depiction of the conspirators as "statesmen and patriots" when in truth they are merely a "pitiful gang of mischief-makers."

Stirling, Brents. " 'Or Else This Were a Savage Spectacle.' " *PMLA* 66 (1951): 765–774. Rpt. rev. in *Unity in Shakespearian Tragedy.* New York: Columbia Univ. Press, 1956. Stirling examines the centrality of ritual and ceremony to the structure of the play. Brutus' efforts to legitimize his political actions through rituals that represent his acts as noble and necessary are countered by Antony's counter-rituals in the second half of the play, exposing and condemning the contradictions in Brutus' idealism.

Velz, John W. "Undular Structure in *Julius Caesar.*" *Modern Language Review* 66 (1971): 21–30. Exploring the marked parallels between the experience and behavior of the play's "successive protagonists," Velz concludes that the play's theme is "the turbulent process by which the commitment of the Romans moved from Pompey to Augustus." The play's presentation of a succession of political rises and falls establishes the theme and gives "unity to this panoramic play."

Memorable Lines

Beware the ides of March.   (BRUTUS   1.2.18)

Why, man, he doth bestride the narrow world
Like a Colossus, and we petty men
Walk under his huge legs and peep about
To find ourselves dishonorable graves.
                      (CASSIUS   1.2.135–138)

Men at some time are masters of their fates.
The fault, dear Brutus, is not in our stars,
But in ourselves, that we are underlings.
                      (CASSIUS   1.2.139–141)

Upon what meat doth this our Caesar feed
That he is grown so great?   (CASSIUS   1.2.149–150)

Let me have men about me that are fat,
Sleek-headed men, and such as sleep o' nights.
Yond Cassius has a lean and hungry look.
He thinks too much. Such men are dangerous.
                      (CAESAR   1.2.192–195)

I rather tell thee what is to be feared
Than what I fear, for always I am Caesar.
                      (CAESAR   1.2.211–212)

But, for mine own part, it was Greek to me.
                      (CASCA   1.2.283–284)

Well, Brutus, thou art noble. Yet I see
Thy honorable mettle may be wrought
From that it is disposed.   (CASSIUS   1.2.308–310)

            What trash is Rome,
What rubbish and what offal, when it serves
For the base matter to illuminate
So vile a thing as Caesar!   (CASSIUS   1.3.108–111)

Th' abuse of greatness is when it disjoins
Remorse from power.   (BRUTUS   2.1.18–19)

But 'tis a common proof
That lowliness is young ambition's ladder.
                                       (BRUTUS   2.1.21–22)

When beggars die there are no comets seen;
The heavens themselves blaze forth the death of princes.
                                       (CALPURNIA   2.2.30–31)

Cowards die many times before their deaths;
The valiant never taste of death but once.
                                       (CAESAR   2.2.32–33)

Danger knows full well
That Caesar is more dangerous than he.   (CAESAR   2.2.44–45)

Et tu, Brutè?   (CAESAR   3.1.78)

How many ages hence
Shall this our lofty scene be acted over
In states unborn and accents yet unknown!
                                       (CASSIUS   3.1.112–114)

O mighty Caesar! Dost thou lie so low?
Are all thy conquests, glories, triumphs, spoils,
Shrunk to this little measure?   (ANTONY   3.1.150–152)

Cry "Havoc!" and let slip the dogs of war.
                                       (ANTONY   3.1.275)

Romans, countrymen, and lovers, hear me for my cause, and
be silent that you may hear.   (BRUTUS   3.2.13–14)

Not that I loved Caesar less, but that I loved Rome more.
                                       (BRUTUS   3.2.21–22)

As he was valiant, I honor him; but, as he was ambitious, I
slew him.   (BRUTUS   3.2.25–27)

Who is here so rude that would not be a Roman? If any, speak, for him have I offended. (BRUTUS 3.2.30–32)

Friends, Romans, countrymen, lend me your ears.
I come to bury Caesar, not to praise him.
(ANTONY 3.2.75–76)

The evil that men do lives after them;
The good is oft interrèd with their bones.
(ANTONY 3.2.77–78)

For Brutus is an honorable man,
So are they all, all honorable men— (ANTONY 3.2.84–85)

Ambition should be made of sterner stuff. (ANTONY 3.2.94)

If you have tears, prepare to shed them now.
(ANTONY 3.2.170)

This was the most unkindest cut of all. (ANTONY 3.2.184)

I come not, friends, to steal away your hearts.
I am no orator, as Brutus is,
But, as you know me all, a plain blunt man.
(ANTONY 3.2.217–219)

For I have neither wit, nor words, nor worth,
Action, nor utterance, nor the power of speech
To stir men's blood. I only speak right on.
(ANTONY 3.2.222–224)

I tell you that which you yourselves do know,
Show you sweet Caesar's wounds, poor poor dumb mouths,
And bid them speak for me. (ANTONY 3.2.225–227)

There is a tide in the affairs of men
Which, taken at the flood, leads on to fortune;
Omitted, all the voyage of their life
Is bound in shallows and in miseries. (BRUTUS 4.3.217–220)

Thou shalt see me at Philippi. (CAESAR'S GHOST 4.3.285)

Forever and forever farewell, Cassius!   (BRUTUS   5.1.120)

O Julius Caesar, thou art mighty yet!
Thy spirit walks abroad and turns our swords
In our own proper entrails.   (BRUTUS   5.3.94–96)

This was the noblest Roman of them all.   (ANTONY   5.5.68)

Contributors

DAVID BEVINGTON, Phyllis Fay Horton Professor of Humanities at the University of Chicago, is editor of *The Complete Works of Shakespeare* (Scott, Foresman, 1980) and of *Medieval Drama* (Houghton Mifflin, 1975). His latest critical study is *Action Is Eloquence: Shakespeare's Language of Gesture* (Harvard University Press, 1984).

DAVID SCOTT KASTAN, Professor of English and Comparative Literature at Columbia University, is the author of *Shakespeare and the Shapes of Time* (University Press of New England, 1982).

JAMES HAMMERSMITH, Associate Professor of English at Auburn University, has published essays on various facets of Renaissance drama, including literary criticism, textual criticism, and printing history.

ROBERT KEAN TURNER, Professor of English at the University of Wisconsin–Milwaukee, is a general editor of the New Variorum Shakespeare (Modern Language Association of America) and a contributing editor to *The Dramatic Works in the Beaumont and Fletcher Canon* (Cambridge University Press, 1966–).

JAMES SHAPIRO, who coedited the bibliographies with David Scott Kastan, is Assistant Professor of English at Columbia University.

❖

JOSEPH PAPP, one of the most important forces in theater today, is the founder and producer of the New York Shakespeare Festival, America's largest and most prolific theatrical institution. Since 1954 Mr. Papp has produced or directed all but one of Shakespeare's plays—in Central Park, in schools, off and on Broadway, and at the Festival's permanent home, The Public Theater. He has also produced such award-winning plays and musical works as *Hair, A Chorus Line, Plenty,* and *The Mystery of Edwin Drood,* among many others.

THE BANTAM SHAKESPEARE COLLECTION

The Complete Works in 28 Volumes

Edited with Introductions by David Bevington

Forewords by Joseph Papp

___ANTONY AND CLEOPATRA 21289-3 $3.95	___FOUR COMEDIES *(The Taming of the Shrew, A Midsummer Night's Dream, The Merchant of Venice, and Twelfth Night)* 21281-8 $4.95
___AS YOU LIKE IT 21290-7 $3.95	
___A COMEDY OF ERRORS 21291-5 $3.95	
___HAMLET 21292-3 $3.95	___THREE EARLY COMEDIES *(Love's Labor's Lost, The Two Gentlemen of Verona, and The Merry Wives of Windsor)* 21282-6 $4.95
___HENRY IV, PART I 21293-1 $3.95	
___HENRY IV, PART II 21294-X $3.95	
___HENRY V 21295-8 $3.95	
___JULIUS CAESAR 21296-6 $3.95	___FOUR TRAGEDIES *(Hamlet, Othello, King Lear, and Macbeth)* 21283-4 $5.95
___KING LEAR 21297-4 $3.95	
___MACBETH 21298-2 $3.95	
___THE MERCHANT OF VENICE 21299-0 $2.95	___HENRY VI, PARTS I, II, and III 21285-0 $4.95
___A MIDSUMMER NIGHT'S DREAM 21300-8 $3.95	___KING JOHN and HENRY VIII 21286-9 $4.95
___MUCH ADO ABOUT NOTHING 21301-6 $3.95	___MEASURE FOR MEASURE, ALL'S WELL THAT ENDS WELL, and TROILUS AND CRESSIDA 21287-7 $4.95
___OTHELLO 21302-4 $3.95	
___RICHARD II 21303-2 $3.95	
___RICHARD III 21304-0 $3.95	
___ROMEO AND JULIET 21305-9 $3.95	___THE LATE ROMANCES *(Pericles, Cymbeline, The Winter's Tale, and The Tempest)* 21288-5 $4.95
___THE TAMING OF THE SHREW 21306-7 $3.95	
___THE TEMPEST 21307-5 $3.95	___THE POEMS 21309-1 $4.95
___TWELFTH NIGHT 21308-3 $3.50	

Ask for these books at your local bookstore or use this page to order.

Please send me the books I have checked above. I am enclosing $____ (add $2.50 to cover postage and handling). Send check or money order, no cash or C.O.D.'s, please.

Name _____

Address _____

City/State/Zip _____

Send order to: Bantam Books, Dept. SH 2, 2451 S. Wolf Rd., Des Plaines, IL 60018
Allow four to six weeks for delivery.
Prices and availability subject to change without notice.

Don't miss these classic tales of
high adventure from master storytellers

____21190-0	CAPTAINS COURAGEOUS,	
	Rudyard Kipling	$2.95/$3.95 in Canada
____21332-6	KIM, Rudyard Kipling	$2.95/$3.50
____21338-5	THE WAR OF THE WORLDS,	
	H. G. Wells	$3.50/not available in Canada
____21011-4	THE RED BADGE OF COURAGE,	
	Stephen Crane	$2.95/$3.95
____21399-7	THE ODYSSEY, Homer	$4.95/$5.95
____21326-1	IVANHOE, Sir Walter Scott	$4.95/$6.95
____21232-X	GULLIVER'S TRAVELS, Jonathan Swift	$3.95/$4.95
____21376-8	THE PHANTOM OF THE OPERA,	
	Gaston Leroux	$4.95/$5.95
____21370-9	THE HUNCHBACK OF NOTRE DAME,	
	Victor Hugo	$4.95/$6.95
____21271-0	DRACULA, Bram Stoker	$3.50/$4.50
____21178-1	PETER PAN, J. M. Barrie	$3.50/$4.50
____21311-3	MOBY DICK, Herman Melville	$3.95/$4.95
____21247-8	FRANKENSTEIN, Mary Shelley	$2.95/$3.95
____21079-3	THE ADVENTURES OF HUCKLEBERRY FINN,	
	Mark Twain	$2.95/$3.95
____21329-6	THE LAST OF THE MOHICANS,	
	James Fenimore Cooper	$4.50/$5.95
____21225-7	THE SEA WOLF, Jack London	$3.95/$4.95

Ask for these books at your local bookstore or use this page to order.

Please send me the books I have checked above. I am enclosing $____ (add $2.50 to cover postage and handling). Send check or money order, no cash or C.O.D.'s, please.

Name _____

Address _____

City/State/Zip _____

Send order to: Bantam Books, Dept. CL 18, 2451 S. Wolf Rd., Des Plaines, IL 60018
Allow four to six weeks for delivery.
Prices and availability subject to change without notice.   CL 18 5/96

From the 1962 New York Shakespeare Festival production of *Julius Caesar*, with Richard Roat as Mark Antony, directed by Joseph Papp at the Heckscher Theater.

THE BANTAM
Shakespeare

JULIUS CAESAR

An exciting new edition of the complete works
of Shakespeare with these features:

·

illustrated with photographs from
New York Shakespeare Festival productions

·

vivid, readable introductions for each play
by noted scholar David Bevington

·

a lively, personal foreword by Joseph Papp

·

an insightful essay on the play in performance

·

modern spelling and punctuation

·

comprehensive source material and scholarship
for each play, with notes

·

up-to-date, annotated bibliographies

·

a convenient listing of key passages

DAVID BEVINGTON, internationally renowned
Shakespeare scholar, is Phyllis Fay Horton Professor
of Humanities at the University of Chicago and editor of
Scott, Foresman's *The Complete Works of Shakespeare.*

JOSEPH PAPP, one of the most important forces
in theater today, is the founder and producer of the New York
Shakespeare Festival, America's largest and most prolific
theatrical institution. He has produced or directed
all but one of Shakespeare's plays.

US $3.95 / $4.95 CAN

ISBN 0-553-21296-6

21296

0 76783 00395 8

S